EYE TO EYE

A JOAN KAHN BOOK

Books by Diana Chang

EYE TO EYE

by

Diana Chang

HARPER & ROW, PUBLISHERS

New York, Evanston, San Francisco, London

FIRST EDITION

Designed by Janice Stern

LIBRARY OF CONGRESS CATALOGING IN PUBLICATION DATA
Chang, Diana
  Eye to eye.
  I. Title.
PZ4.C4557Ey [PS3553.H272]   813'.5'4   74–4857
ISBN 0–06–010704–9

The technique of psychoanalysis as we know it at present was born as a hunch about the essential nature of the dream and the neuroses. The simple and leading thought, which seems to be so near now and was so far from the minds of Freud's contemporaries, is that men reveal themselves—all their emotional secrets—when they talk freely about themselves; not just when they talk about their secrets, but about everything concerning themselves. They give away what bothers them, disturbs and torments them, all that occupies their thoughts and arouses their emotions—even when they would be most unwilling to talk directly about these things.

Freud has said that mortals are not made to keep a secret and that self-betrayal oozes from all their pores.

—*Theodor Reik,* Listening with the Third Ear

In sum, the reality of art remains a subjective reality, the reality of creating it.

In Surealist doctrin, the real is surreal, hence fantasy is everywhere.

Harold Rosenberg in The New Yorker

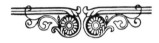

I see! At last I see! I am a visual artist, successful, ambitious, a passionate man. (My stuff is in museums.) I feel in my bones my life is going to go full tilt ahead on all levels to even greater heights.

I was that withdrawn George Safford. You too will see as I tell my story that I was somewhat detached, a little withdrawn. Be patient with my defensive self, as Emerson was, Dr. Emerson to whom I owe so much. Dr. Emerson too failed to see something important—that we were involved in a bizarre triangle! *Him!* Impossible to believe!

I, a visual artist, did not see very well. He, Dr. Emerson, a perceptive, intuitive headshrinker, did not perceive until halfway through my story. Isn't life stranger, more ironic, than anyone can imagine? Isn't what happened to me, to us, a kind of metaphor of the ambiguities of reality? What was Dr. Emerson's relationship to me anyway? Are we all blind? And most passing strange of all, it is Dr. Emerson who needs me now!

I am excited, but I must start calmly at the beginning. I am the new George Safford, but I must show as objectively as possible how I used to be. I will relive my analysis as I relived my life when I was being analyzed. I will show exactly how I was—unseeing, laughable, in pain.

This is my story of being hung up on lovesickness—*all the while* I was making art which told me exactly what my trouble was. I actually did not understand what I was creating while I was creating it. Feeling has a compulsive drive to become form, *even if you don't understand the source of the feeling.* I can't get over how we all create our lives, for better or worse, out of our feelings. In that sense, everyone is an artist.

I know Dr. Emerson would agree with me there. Everyone's life *is* his work of art.

I have to start with Bob Meacham. We met in the rain at an artists' colony in Vermont. We were both a lot younger then, in our middle twenties. We've been friends almost twelve years, eleven for sure anyway. Bob was married then; I wasn't. Then I got married and stayed married. Bob is now unmarried, but he is not strictly speaking single, which I profoundly regret. He may not get the girl; no. But he thinks he's got her, which would be good enough for him. He's always been the secure one.

I was troubled for a long time before I knew I was troubled. I was tense and agitated for four months before Bob referred me to Dr. Emerson.

About a year and a half ago, in July, when my firm, Party Packages, was just getting on the map and I was designing paper tablecloths with turkeys and Pilgrim hats for Thanksgiving and the museums were, at the same time, sending people over to look at my other work (my real work, the scenes), I was already involved with Nan Weil. She wasn't involved with me yet, but I was involved with her, and keeping the thing a dark secret from my wife, Edith, of course. I would work, and shake; work some more and shake some more. Bob was over at the loft kibitzing, as we say in New York. He is an associate professor of English and a poet and was on his summer vacation of three solid months, a stretch of time that appalls my self-employed heart. Anyway, having nothing better to do, he hung around the shop. Every so often, passing him where he was perched on a high stool, I went to the front door to watch or to listen—or so it appeared to Bob. My office or shop or studio or loft (it is all these things) is on the second floor of a professional building in the mid-Fifties off Second Avenue. A steep flight of stairs leads past my door to two other floors where six people have their offices. I am the only one with a floor through. Beneath me is a Jewish delicatessen with the best half-sour pickles in town.

"You waiting for someone special?" Bob asked.

"Me?" I said scornfully. I wanted him to realize he couldn't be more wrong.

"Edith says you're nervous, overworking."

"She's crazy."

"All this commercial stuff is going to destroy you."

I always knew Bob was contemptuous of money, of my having formed Party Packages, my very own firm, three years before. But then he doesn't have a family to support. He doesn't even have to pay toward his son's maintenance, because he has the luck to have an ex-wife whose new husband won't let Bob contribute to the boy's support. Ellen, when she married again, chose a responsible man, a pediatrician.

"You stick to your poetry," I said.

"You're driving yourself too hard. Why kill yourself to be a lousy millionaire someday! You'll end up with ulcers and shattered nerves."

"Nothing's wrong with my nerves!"

I was moving back and forth, trying not to step on a fifteen-by-twenty-five-foot tablecloth. My girl Friday, a fiftyish workhorse who is stenographer-bookkeeper-receptionist, was by the window. My partner—the business end of Party Packages, Inc.—was as usual out selling. It has been my practice, as soon as I have several designs worked out and accepted by buyers, to get in free-lance artists, mostly recent graduates of Cooper Union. We then plunge in and work like devils, morning, noon and night, turning out offsets and prints until the orders are completed. But that day only Miss Price was around.

Apparently I went to the door again, shook some more and, in turning back, upset a can of acrylic paint. I cried out as if stabbed, threw whatever I could lay hands on at no one in particular, and then, to save face, I suppose, and to collect myself, I declared in high dudgeon (all this is as later described by Bob), "It's past two and high time I had something to eat!" Miss Price crouched over her work, looking chastened, and I threw myself down the stairs and was later joined by Bob over a hot pastrami.

Bob has a slightly bloated face but eyes that listen like a child's. Those listening eyes of his—they are all ears. But I never told him about Nan Weil. I really am an honorable man. About two weeks later even I noticed I was shaking. Anything I held in my hands shook. Paper, and I handle a lot of it, thin and heavy, rumbled lightly like the faintest thunder. I couldn't think or follow a problem through with my usual efficiency; I felt I wasn't on top of anything. Yet I was still working and eating as usual. (It's just occurred to me: Bob has no trouble *seeing* all he needs to see.)

Several weeks later, maybe it was in September, I lost my appetite. I'm thin and bony, towheaded and look both older than thirty-seven and younger. People with my kind of metabolism almost always look younger, since we don't thicken into middle age, but my face looked older to me. The lines on the sides of my mouth began to look sunken in and hard. I was so thin my joints were knobby.

Edith, my wife, who is so extraordinarily ordinary in herself and so suited to me, had suggested several times I see our doctor. "I don't think you're well, sweetie."

After several of her attempts to get me to go and visit our internist (who in my father's day would have been called a general practitioner as he had been), she handed me a scrap of paper with Bob's handwriting on it. I didn't even look at it. Recognizing his hand was enough.

"So you discussed me, you two did!"

She was slow to defend herself, which is her problem. "I'm sorry, but I was worried about you. He was too, and so, yes, I'm sorry, we did discuss you."

"Why don't you two mind your own business!"

"Sweetie—"

"Don't you sweetie me, damn you!" My nerves were truly shot.

"I'm sorry." I did not find it out of keeping that she should apologize for having simply been concerned. She also looked hurt, again a part of her problem.

"Don't you ever sweetie me again!" She filled me with guilt, and I was already overflowing with it. I was in love with Nan, and here was my wife trying to take care of me. She was really making life unbearable. (I was so irascible!)

But a week later, when I felt positively ill and since my partner insisted (and I do have a practical head on me), I did go to our doctor. He examined me thoroughly, asked several questions I found unnecessary and impertinent, and recommended a psychiatrist, a Dr. Wright. Our doctor was very matter-of-fact—he said he referred many patients to psychiatrists. He kept a list of six names and Dr. Wright, in his opinion, was the one for me.

When I got home I reluctantly admitted to Edith that I realized I had to talk to someone. (Thank God, I did! I bless her for insisting!) I told her I was torn because of party packaging on the one hand and fine art work on the other. (Of course, I knew it was Nan I had to talk to someone about, and I was strangely relieved I could apparently put it off no longer.) Edith was happy again. We were very tender with each other that evening, and then she took out that scrap of paper again. In Bob's writing, it said, "Dr. Yale H. Emerson, 154–1702."

"I'll never get used to these new phone numbers," I said. "Why can't it be Lackawanna four or whatever?"

"Bob was really worried. He's so sweet. He got the name from the Steins."

"Why should I see this guy? I got this other name today."

"It's up to you, sweetie."

"Who are the Steins?"

"She's the girl who teaches poetry and used to be a student of Bob's and whose brother is a psychologist? They, the Steins, that is, live in West Orange."

"How do I know he's any good?"

"They consult, I understand. I mean, you go once and then he decides whether or not you're his kind of case. You don't have to like him either, of course. That's called a consultation. You could, I suppose, see them both."

"Dr. Yale Harvard Emerson."

Edith laughed. She laughs easily, readily, delightfully, her rather ordinary face breaking up into new arrangements, as when the colored bits in a kaleidoscope slide a mere eighth of an inch and the parts "smile" into another pattern. By ordinary, I mean white Protestant, like myself. Edith Shaw Safford is five-five, smooth-limbed, average full-breasted, blue-eyed dark blond, tans handsomely. She could be from California, and if she were, she'd at once evoke beaches, orange juice and an openness, but not a commitment, to Zen or any other philosophy that was making the rounds. If she were from Kansas, she'd suggest fields of wheat, white shingle houses and music sororities. Actually, she is a born and bred New Yorker, and I love her because she is quite beautiful in this ordinariness I share with her. She could be the girl who runs toward you in the commercials with her clean hair flying out slowly behind her, confident because she's used the right deodorant. Edith also has an upper-class aura, though she's middle class. Her father owns an East Side pharmacy (but one which eschews carrying paperbacks and ice cream cones) with a rich clientele. She went to Smith, might aspire to B. H. Wragge clothes but is happier in Swedish cottons. My wife is really lovely, but the old George P. Safford was out of his head with desire for Nan Weil. What an agony that was!

"How do you know H stands for Harvard?"

"It just has to," I said.

"I like Yale Harvard Emerson," she said.

"Yeah, but he may not like me."

"I mean I like his name. Go see them both," she said with uncharacteristic authority. Though that is only half true. She can be quite adamant and brook no challenging of her attitudes. She is for everything from civil rights, recycling, buckling one's seat belt and not exterminating city pigeons, to self-determination in both Vietnams. I may sound slightly facetious, but I know I am like her all the way down the line; and I don't mean anything more than that, like lots of people, we're liberal, versatile, and walking hodgepodges of virtue, applied and applied again. Not, mind you, that there's anything wrong with this.

"Yale is a peculiar first name. Can you imagine calling a son of ours Penn State?"

"That's not analogous at all," she said. "It's more like calling a girl Smith than City College."

"Smith Safford sounds rich and beautiful," I said.

"Let's call our next girl Smith for the old alma mater." We have a daughter about whom I am rarely troubled—she's a perfect little girl. I call her Puttykins; Edith refers to her as the daughter; her name is Amanda. She is three and a half now, long-legged, and looks like both of us, that is, totally correct, white Protestant and turning into a miniature movie actress. Not the sexpot type but the serious kind, like Eva Marie Saint or a less flinchingly sensitive Geraldine Page. That's how Puttykins will turn out, I'm convinced. I rarely worry about her though. She simply doesn't figure in my problems, at least as they have been revealed to me.

"His middle name may not be Harvard at all."

"I never said it was," but I had been the one to mock his name. "It could be anything. That H could stand for anything," I said lamely. I was beginning to shake again. Thinking of undergoing analysis, being content with Edith, all the while knowing how I felt about Nan Weil, made me shake all over. I was suffering from a kind of dislocation.

I was already terrified of seeing Dr. Emerson, already resisting.

"Do Yale locks have Yale keys?"

"Yale keys?" I cried out in mortal terror.

Later on I said to myself, It's kismet. He will unlock my problem. I have always finally faced my fears. I require it of myself. I am Calvinist that way. So I chose to go to Dr. Emerson instead of Dr. Wright because his name was Yale. Is that a good reason? If his name had simply been John Adams Emerson, I would have gone to Dr. Wright in the first place and had my head shrunk with no extra ado. Heaven help us all. It turned out the H stood for Herbert. Herbert, believe it or not! My middle name is Peter. George Peter Safford. That combination of names connotes me. It boggles the mind. Just being me, this mess of experience which is me, my living self, boggles my mind. My self boggles its mind. Think of it. It was this thinking about myself that I could never quite get used to. Who (I) was thinking of what (self)? I was thinking of me. No wonder I sometimes felt I'd get nowhere. But how glad I am I've learned what I learned! I am quite earnest when you get right down to it. It's only the final turn of the screw I now lament.

I pulled myself together, called Dr. Emerson, told him the indirect manner in which I'd got his name, even blurted out that I'd selected him over Dr. Wright, and told him who I was. I remember insisting, as though he cared then, "My work is neither painting nor sculpture. I want you to know I'm not a painter or sculptor. I'm an artist in the visual field. I am a visual artist." This didn't throw him; he didn't object at all, and he gave me my first appointment.

Edith was very happy those first weeks. She watched my appetite (saw that it improved ever so slightly) and kept Amanda out of my way when she felt I was getting edgy. I wasn't home much, what with the big Thanksgiving campaign and my poking around stores weekends for things I needed for a scene I was creating. For their new show the Guggenheim had recently purchased a weathered porch I was particularly satisfied with. Needless to say, I was thrilled the Guggenheim Museum was beginning to collect my work, and they don't usually go for my sort of thing, either, but I did not say I was thrilled. I remember saying to Emerson, "I am gratified." I must have sounded like a prig! These metaphors I make were beginning to send the critics, and I thought what I felt was gratification!

I liked Dr. Emerson at once. I had this weird sense of meeting myself over his desk. When I told him this later, he said it wasn't strange, that it was part of the idea, but that it took with me rather immediately. While I will declare he said this or that, I can never be absolutely certain he actually put anything in so many words. It's hard to remember conversations a week old, not to mention a year or more old. Since these conversations were of such importance to me, one might mistakenly think I'd remember every word and how the exchanges went. I never did lie down, by the way. Don't know why, but I never did, is all. There's a couch in his office, but he never suggested I take to it, and I never moved toward it myself. Were we both waiting for the other to make the first move? Surely, if he had thought it would have helped me, he would have suggested that I try it—it would have been his professional duty. But he never did. I never thought I really wanted to. I thought I was quite unrepressed. Actually, I was scared. Oh yes, quite scared.

Sometimes he only *seemed* to say something, which I'd then think about or act on as if he had actually said it. It was always my own judgment, my own choices being exercised. Other times he'd guide me toward saying something or thinking something myself, and I could feel his deliberate guiding mind. If I'd ask, "Am I right about that?" he'd often throw the whole thing back on me by replying, "In terms of your problem . . ."

"My problem is Nan," I'd say. "I've got to get her, so I know where I stand." I had the feeling he did not find this out of line. Nothing I said, no desire I expressed, was out of line.

When I entered his office the first time, Dr. Emerson greeted me with a firm handshake. I had arrived there ten minutes too early and sat waiting, biting the inside of my mouth. He must have two reception rooms or another exit, I remember thinking, for I heard a little activity on the other side of the heavy door, but no one, no patient, that is, emerged. Instead, the door opened, and this tall man with a surprisingly youthful face asked me in.

"I got here too early," I declared too emphatically.

"Sit down, Mr. Safford," he said while he stepped behind his desk to adjust a Venetian blind.

I did not add, I got here too early to prove to you I'm a responsible man who is prompt and businesslike. I'm not erratic like the rest of the people who have to see you. (See how defensive I was!)

"You know the Steins," he said, looking at a memo pad.

"Who?" I asked, stupid.

"The Steins referred you to me."

Now he's going to think I'm paralyzed with nervousness, I thought. To make up for my slowness, I spoke very fast. "No, no, the Steins are friends of a friend of mine, Bob Meacham. They probably gave him your name, or rather Dorothy Stein's brother, who is a psychologist, probably gave him your name. Dorothy, before she became Dorothy Stein, was a student of and who knows what else to Bob Meacham, this poet I know. Then he gave it to me, or rather to Edith." I stopped. "Edith is my wife."

He smiled slightly, just like people, I thought. I tried to imagine him making love or eating breakfast or taking a piece of gum off the bottom of his shoe. But I wasn't successful.

"You said over the phone you'd been to your internist, your doctor, and he recommended someone else. I know nothing about you obviously, and your internist knows you well enough to have recommended a particular psychiatrist to you, so perhaps this meeting of ours is simply exploratory."

I was certain he was only talking to cover up his real activity: taking me in to see how far gone I was. Of course, I'm putting on a bit about this, but part of me did think this way. I must be entirely accurate. Of course, a lot I don't remember. I simply do not remember how it went or what he said exactly. But I must emphasize that I'm also fabricating nothing, for I must tell what happened as clearly and as wholly as is humanly possible. I am human, humanly, humanest. I am very human. My sessions with Dr. Emerson made me realize just how human I am. I always knew I was human, but not quite that human. No, not quite that human. But it's nothing to be ashamed of. It's not out of line to be very human.

In fact, I met myself there in his office simply as a human being— not as a husband, a father, a potential lover, a son, a friend, a partner at Party Packages, an artist, an A student, a consumer or a credit card holder. I was just a human being in the raw, or almost in the raw. I clutched several figurative fig leaves against my body, which, as the jargon has it, defined my problem. And Dr. Emerson grew to know exactly what I was hiding by the position of the fig leaves. Something like that. But it was not his method to tear the leaves off by main force.

The stance I took that first day, leaning back in the chair, my hands carefully unclenched, my legs crossed easily, was calculated to calm me and to impress him. (Has my defensiveness been apparent to everyone else all my life? God! I cringe. I was the last to see it!)

"Would you like a . . ." he said, leaning forward to offer me a cigarette.

"I don't smoke," I lied. If I picked up a cigarette, he'd see the way my hands shook. I leaned back farther.

"If you don't mind," he said, lighting one up himself. Then, without thinking, I leaned forward; he fumbled for and offered the package again, and I snatched a cigarette out of it. He realized I'd lied, and I knew that he noticed my hand shaking. He saw I saw what he saw. Eye to eye we were beginning to see.

Then the silent treatment started.

In a way I found that silence beautiful. Even when it felt like a cruelty, a kind of reversed third degree—painful in its very lack of force, in its maniacal permissiveness. That silence reminds me of the best parts of childhood. Rain and warmth. Or snow and sleepiness and milk just before being tucked into bed. Knowing that a grownup is nearby before plunging into the pool. The sharing of a deep rich idiotic secret with another kid.

I didn't know I thought the silence beautiful that first day. I blinked, I puffed, I stubbed out the cigarette, I avoided his eyes.

He finally said gently (maybe it was only fifteen seconds later), "This is just a consultation. What did you want to see me about?"

"My name is George P. Safford. I'm thirty-six, an artist—a visual artist—married. I have a daughter and I make good money."

Dr. Emerson has a funny look around his eyes. He's since told me he wears contact lenses, which might or might not account for the look. He stares, or looks as if he's staring. Every so often he opens his eyes very wide as if to adjust the lenses. Only I didn't know then he wore them, so he seemed to dilate like a kindly fish coming up to me at regular intervals. When he opened his eyes wide, he looked closer, then he'd recede and keep a natural distance. He emanated a great gentleness (not tenderness, which would not do), a presence of just being there, but really being there, all yours if you'd only have the wit to give or to take, which could be interchangeable.

"Is this the first time you've seen a psychiatrist?"

"Nothing has ever been wrong with me. I'm absolutely fine," I said. The man didn't laugh!

"This is just a consultation. Why did you want to see me?" There was absolutely no insistence in his tone. He was only creating a limbo in which I could swim or drown.

"You seem so young!" I complained. I thought, He's much too young. Dr. Wright is probably bearded like Freud. But Dr. Wright could be wrong, or too right. In the state I was in, I was superstitious about names, symbols, everything.

"I'm fully qualified," he said.

"Of course, I'm the first to realize age has nothing to do with it," I said reasonably. "I had my first one-man show at twenty-three."

I let that sink in. It made me feel better that he knew specifically what I had done in the great world outside this quiet, oh too quiet, room.

"Maybe it's my success that's unnerving me," I said very earnestly. (Still he didn't laugh.) "I'm quite successful. After you've been used to struggling, success can feel very unreal, and that feeling of unreality can undo you. I mean, there is in everyone a need to suffer, don't you think? Dostoevsky explored this, and others, lots of others, I can't even think who, so many did. I don't get around to reading much actually." I didn't know where those words came from; I started talking, being creative verbally, and enjoyed it. I realized there was a contradiction in what I'd said, and I'd just started, so I had better be careful. I'd just told him I'd had a one-man show at twenty-three and yet I spoke of success after great struggle. Therefore, I hurriedly seized on Blake to talk about, Blake whom I only faintly remembered from college reading. I went on about the creative process at some length. From Blake I went on to quote, " 'Success is counted sweetest by those who ne'er succeed. To comprehend a nectar requires sorest need,' " and supplied, "My mother quotes a lot of poetry. She once gave an Emily Dickinson reading in her younger days. Personally I don't care for her poetry," but in the back of my mind I was thinking other things. (All that cerebrating I used to do was part of my problem. I was all mind, thinking overtime.) I thought, Nan Weil is the nectar, and my need is dreadfully sore. But I mustn't give myself away to this Dr. Emerson. I was talking so dangerously close to the truth. My need was killing me. I love you, Nan. Save me, Nan. But while I am in this office, let me hang on to my mind, my intelligence, my wits.

"You speak of struggle," he said, "yet it appears you've done remarkably well, and you are only thirty-six now."

I looked at him balefully. I didn't find him so good-looking at this point, but respect was sneaking in the back door. If I hadn't known he was an analyst or psychiatrist or psychologist (the field is confusing to laymen), I'd have taken him for the urbane executive of an imaginative public relations firm or a professor of, say, mathematics at a radically liberal arts college. He was both pragmatic and open-minded, I felt, banking rather heavily on my intuitions. After all, he'd only spoken a handful of sentences so far. But today I agree with myself. Emerson *is* both pragmatic and open-ended in his approach to me, to Nan and to himself. Remarkable how right my intuitions can be. Remarkable, considering. The partially blind see some things quite clearly!

"I'm not trying to trip you up," he said evenly. "But you did say you had a one-man show at twenty-three, or did I misunderstand?"

"You talk more than I thought you would," I countered. "Do analysts *talk* to their patients?"

13

"I'm fully qualified," he said with a slight smile.

"In other words, you do know what you're doing."

"I think so."

That, for some reason, I found hilarious. The way he said it. My making him say it. I started laughing and had a hard time stopping.

Maybe I was a bit hysterical. Or maybe he made me feel whimsical, witty. I am telling it as it was.

I collected myself, trying to make out what he thought of my laughter (either "Anyone with such a magnificent sense of humor must be normal" or "He's cracking up right in front of me"), and continued: "My problem is the problem most artists face at one time or another. I'm a fine artist, making the bulk, but not all, of my living at something I don't respect very much. Believe me, it's a common problem among creative people, and I just need to talk to someone qualified, like yourself," I put in generously, "to resolve and accept these facts of life. I have a family to support, after all, and since I'm the responsible type, and knowing I've made my bed, I just want to feel happier lying in it, so to speak." The bed I wanted to lie in was Nan Weil's. God, who is deaf and mute, what was I to do! I wasn't lying to Dr. Emerson. I was really very honest, honest I certainly was, I persuaded myself. "I am quite realistic and mature. On top of everything else, I am also a good husband and father." I believe my head was tilted arrogantly as I claimed this.

"What physical symptoms have you had recently?" he asked.

Still thinking of Nan, I blurted out, "I keep going to the door. Bob noticed." I realized I had made a mistake the moment I said it.

"Bob?"

"He's the one who gave me your name." Then I fell to describing Bob in detail. (I doubt that Dr. Emerson remembers any of this. I sincerely hope not. I don't want Dr. Emerson to be hurt, ever.) I never knew I had so many details about Bob stored in my head. I was able to go on about him much longer than I had been able to about William Blake. I didn't want Dr. Emerson to get back to the door I mentioned or to physical ailments.

14

"Bob Meacham always gets the girls; it's remarkable how they go for him. And he doesn't give them a line at all. That's the whole point. He doesn't need them, so they flock around like birds. Have you noticed that the English call their girls birds? At least they do in their movies. Bob has great power over the female of the species; he has that magnetism, that charisma, which I've never had. But then, I don't need it. I'm very happily married.

"Some successful actors, performers, political figures have that charisma. These people are sure of themselves, and people are attracted to sureness. People in general aren't sure of themselves and seek those who are. I've watched Bob with girls over the years. He's nice, considerate, all that, but he belongs to his work first of all and secondly to the girl. She senses this and it drives her up the wall. I mean, it drives her mad with passion. It isn't that he's cold, remote, unkind. And I don't mean to say the girls are masochistic. They simply sense that he's secure with an inner security. He belongs to himself. To his work. Actually, he's quite selfish in that sense. But his work is important to him, as it should be. I think—don't you agree? —that a man's work is possibly the most important aspect of his life. My work, I must say, is exceedingly important to me." I felt safe again, having brought the subject back to my work, away from the door. I continued: "I have always been a hard worker, at whatever I've done. I feel rarefied after a good day's work. It's a great feeling."

Dr. Emerson had dilated his eyes, blinked and stirred a little in his chair during my dissertation on Bob. "Besides going compulsively to the door, as you put it, what other physical symptoms have you had?"

He demonstrated that he couldn't be thrown off the track. This tall, youngish, sober, unperturbable headshrinker probably did know what he was doing. And I was never so crazy as not really to want to be helped. I decided to come clean.

"I shake," I said, my voice full of candor. But he already knew that from watching me with the cigarette, so I wasn't coming clean after all. I hung on to my cleverness for weeks, I might add.

"Another cigarette?" He proffered the pack.

15

"You see I shake," I said, taking the cigarette and demonstrating my shakes with a certain swagger. It felt good to shake openly. For weeks I'd been trying to control and hide my shaking.

He nodded. "Do you sleep?"

I nodded.

"As usual?"

I nodded up and down, but then the direction of my head changed until I was nodding yes from side to side.

"Not as usual?"

"I wake up different."

He waited for me to elaborate, but I didn't.

"Eat?"

I decided I'd better tell him the truth. He might phone Edith (Who knew, maybe analysts checked?), and she'd tell him anyway. "I have no appetite."

"Have you lost weight?"

"Yes." Twenty pounds to be exact. And I was thin to begin with.

"What would you say—our time is almost up—was bothering you the most?"

"The shakes," I said. "These shakes. They notice at work. I handle a lot of paper. I don't want my partner to think I'm not holding up my end of things."

"I meant— What would you say your problem was at this given moment?"

"Oh, that. Well, my way of making a living—and it promises to become even better—is in conflict with my real interest, in which I am also very successful and I think getting more so." He really didn't even allow himself to smile—that remarkable man.

"I suggest, Mr. Safford, you come and see me next Tuesday, and then we can decide what other day of the week we can set up."

"What other day . . ." I repeated stupidly.

"Twice a week would be best. Tuesdays and then one other day. We'll see."

"Oh, you—" No, it would not be right somehow to say, Oh, you want me as a patient. After all, I had some say in this too.

"You mean," I started, "we're going to . . ."

"Think it over. Consult the other psychiatrist, if you like, and then decide whether or not you are coming back to me next week. If you aren't coming, call me as soon as possible."

"You think I need analysis?" I asked bleakly.

"Two sessions a week does not necessarily constitute analysis."

"You think I need to see you?" I rephrased it.

"No one can say that but the patient himself. Consult the other psychiatrist, if you like, Mr. Safford." He had stood up, and now I stood up, and we moved toward a door I hadn't noticed before, which opened directly into the apartment house lobby. Before we reached the door, my eye caught sight of two paintings on either side of it. Dr. Emerson extended his hand and shook mine firmly.

"Tuesday at two," he said.

"Good-by, sir," I said, as if he were old and bearded. Actually, I don't think he's much more than forty.

His taste in painting is pitiful, I thought. He obviously hasn't seen enough, but still the one on the right was not bad for abstract expressionism as done by a second-rater. Pleasant reds and browns. Warm, expressive, with a certain breadth of vision. But not first rate. And besides, it was abstract expressionism, and I had been through that school for some time, but personally and for good.

I felt happy though to realize he collected real live paintings. Most doctors didn't get beyond prints. On the strength of his interest in art, I didn't consult with Dr. Wright but returned to Dr. Yale H. Emerson, and so our involvement, which was to turn out so bizarrely (there is no other word for it), began. Maybe he would know more about my psyche than I, but I knew two fair-to-middling paintings when I looked at them. I thought in those early days of my analysis I had eyes which saw.

17

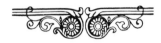

I don't remember his calling me Mr. Safford ever again, but he also never said George. Or am I making this up? It seems to me he never did. In order to reduce me to my nameless self? Or did something happen to me when I entered that quiet room, that not-so-large but seemingly limitless space at the butt end of my thoughts where the beginnings lay? I made the basketball team in high school, so I'm not short. But there were times in those sessions I felt so small and helpless; other times I was an enormity of insight and surmise—my thinking enmeshed the whole world. Still other times I felt shrunken to my real self, and liberated. I felt discrete, shrunken to size, yet more powerful, more in charge than when I was continuous, extended and forfeited through others.

I suppose it's nothing to be wondered at. I mean, it is the purpose behind the whole blamed tedious process. I really gave him the business those first three weeks.

For six or more sessions I talked about my work, my work habits, my discovering when I was twelve I wanted to be a painter, my development from primitive through abstract, to pop and a montage effect I believed I could have called my own at one time, through what is now referred to as color field, though I was doing it when it had no name. Its namelessness (like my own with Dr. Emerson) was a condition which was destroyed as soon as the effect was named and therefore freed. In the case of that kind of painting, naming it made it marketable and copyable.

"I have a certain genius," I remember telling him. "I am always onto something new. I don't mean because I am eager to be avant-garde. I simply *am* avant-garde. I can't help it. All I want is to get 'it,' that something, and then go on. My genius lies in the fact that what I want turns out to be the next thing. It's quite remarkable." I watched his face closely. I concluded that he did not want to betray his admiration for me lest it inhibit me from talking further, so I obliged him by continuing without his encouragement. He said almost nothing for three sessions. During the fourth and fifth sessions he seemed impatient, but I refused to let it affect my train of thought. After all, it was my analysis or psychotherapy or whatever, not his, and my money was paying for it.

It amuses me. The whole bit. I thought this then.

I mean, The whole bit is a farce, I said to myself.

Life is a laugh. And I was the laughingstock. I was inflexible and mocking—unconsciously. I was afraid.

"So far," he pointed out the next time, as if I weren't perfectly well aware of it, "you've talked about nothing but your work. This is our sixth session."

"But if I can just tell you all about it, I'll stop shaking. I am certain of it. My latest phase, I feel, is positively it, though I have to admit" —I was always careful to be reasonable, the sign of a secure man— "I've thought this is it every time I've settled into a style, a genre. I think I simply go through phases faster than others. I was a primitive in high school—"

"You've already told me that," he broke in for the first time.

"—an abstract expressionist during and after college, and went into pop and an erased-montage effect when I was around twenty-four and until I was twenty-nine. Then I simplified my colors and abstracted from abstraction itself. I know this is Greek to the layman, but anyway the erased effect and the color field I reached just one step ahead of the others. I don't say others were not feeling their way toward it across the country and even in Australia, Japan and Israel, but the point is I was just one step ahead (as were some others) and by the time we pioneers consolidated our thinking in that style, everyone else was in it. They came to it from the outside, so to speak. They jumped on the bandwagon and produced it professionally. I had got to it differently, from the inside out. I'd gone through each phase to evolve into the one ahead. My development as a total person coincided with my work and vice versa. But I'm politic too. It goes without saying

19

you can't keep changing and keep a gallery or a following. After my first couple of shows as a young painter, I didn't really stand up to be counted until I reached the color field stage. Now I'm doing these scenes I've told you about. In a way, I'm more a sculptor than a painter. If I didn't have my hands full with Party Packages, I'd be working on several scenes at once. I think. Though I'm always working on them in my head, if you know what I mean. I'm always thinking." (As if he didn't know.) I wound down like an old gramophone, which reminded me of something.

"That reminds me. I'm planning to put an old gramophone in my next set. It's to be a period piece."

"I saw the . . . the arrangement at the Guggenheim," he said softly. I felt shaken.

"You . . . you did?" I asked blankly.

I couldn't believe my ears. He, Dr. Emerson, had taken himself to the Guggenheim to look at my work! Why, it was like learning that a character in fiction like Camille or Captain Ahab had shopped at the A & P yesterday. My head swam. There was nothing fictional about either him or me or the Guggenheim. What was the matter with me? The museum was about five blocks from where I sat. He could easily drop in during his lunch hour. I tried to recover my sense of reality.

"It's a period piece," he commented. "But recent."

"How did you like it?" I beamed.

"It's strangely real," he said.

"Thank you," I said with heartfelt gratitude.

"I didn't say I liked it."

"Oh." I was felled like a young tree with one blow.

"Surely, you are certain of its value . . ."

The arrangement, as he called it, is titled "The Porch." What would he know of metaphors? I said to myself then. It is the life-size replica (though something is wrong with this word here) of a weathered porch on which there are several objects: a high-backed dated-looking bamboo and wicker chair, a sandbox, a lighted lamp inside a right-hand side window, evidence of life inside the living room, and two doors. The house door itself is opened flat against the wall of the hallway. The screen door is slightly ajar and opens outward, suggesting that someone or a presence has just entered or exited or perhaps is still standing there invisible. Through touches of faded color, peeled paint, careful spacing of objects, and traces of sand almost imperceptibly sifting across the porch (I have an electric fan turning slowly behind the façade), I created a mood of waiting. No, not so much waiting as of the postponement of a beginning.

"Did you notice," I asked, "that the sand accumulates under and around the chair, and there is no trace of feet having scuffled it? Did you see?" I asked him.

"It is strangely real," he said. "I did not say I did not like it."

I began to beam again. "I feel I have really found my medium. What would you say the period was?"

"What had you intended?"

"Nineteen forty-one, to be precise," I said at once.

"You were exactly three years old," he rejoined, seeing something himself.

I don't think I even heard him. Yet I remember he did say that to me.

"My next piece is going back farther. I'm planning to get in this gramophone, some turn-of-the-century valentines framed and a hope chest."

"I would say supper was over," he said.

I looked at him. I didn't understand. Could it be he was still on my porch?

"Why would I, at the museum, get the impression supper was over?" he asked.

"The dining room is in the dark," I supplied.

"I would guess it must be after eight o'clock," he said. "And if there are any people around, they might now be in the living room."

"It's crazy, isn't it?" I cried. "How *real* art is. I mean, here you are making up a story about a . . . a scene of mine. You're making up a story about a made-up piece of art. You're talking as if it's a real porch. We sold it for eight thousand dollars, can you believe it!"

"Real estate values are not our concern here."

"I mean the museum paid me eight thousand for it."

"You know you are successful, yet you can't quite believe it," he said.

"Eight thousand dollars," I went on, "for a pile of junk I collected here and there, or bought from my mother, and I get eight thousand dollars for it right off the bat. But the way you do it—that touch of genius—is what counts. You see, you've read into it that supper was over. So 'The Porch' really works. The metaphor works. I'm nuts for metaphors." I contemplated my own powers. "What do you really think of this kind of art? I mean, it's kind of crazy, isn't it?"

"No," he said. Just no. Dr. Emerson obviously couldn't talk about art, I thought, and I bet when he goes to the movies he sees life, a slice of life, and interprets that very well, at a high level, of course. When I go to see a movie, I see a slice of life too, but I bring my eyes as well as my understanding to it. I see an art form, an object, a new event inventing itself. The way a movie is done is as much its meaning as the story itself. Sometimes I go just to see moving pictures, I mean, pictures that move. Art is not only a representation of reality; it takes its place in reality too and can be a representation of itself representing itself. It doesn't have to mean anything necessarily. The effect is enough for me.

"But it *is* crazy," I insisted. "To be paid for making scenes. You know what the expression 'making a scene' means. But that is what I do—I create scenes."

"It's literary," he said. "I'd say your work in the visual field is literary in essence."

How perceptive, I thought, not really perceiving what he was saying but enjoying myself thoroughly. So I was literary as well. Well, what do you know, I said to myself, he says I'm literary.

"You are trying to say something through your work."

"Well, naturally, that's the whole point," I said with ill-concealed irascibility. Of course I was trying to say something through my work. Trying to create an atmosphere, to stay a moment in time, to hold it there to be felt and relived by thousands of people. I mean, really, how banal could he be? But it was I who did not see what he saw.

"I have always tried to say something through my work," I said. "If it were just a matter of copying myself (of course, I mean this in a special sense), I'd still be turning out large red and pink canvases. I did well in that too, you know."

I left him that day feeling flat as after a party which had never got off the ground. It made me wonder about the science of psychoanalysis or psychiatry or whatever I was undergoing. I was giving Dr. Emerson the benefit of the doubt; but I thought, There are no magicians anywhere, decidedly not.

The next time I belabored him some more about work. About work in general, this time, and its importance to the male of the human species. "I think a man's work, whatever it may be, is the most important single factor in his life. Wouldn't you say so too?"

He shifted in his chair and wouldn't give me the time of day. He didn't answer.

I went on: "I was never one of those artists who lean on a woman financially and then hate her for becoming realistic. I know a lot of people involved in situations like this. Maybe I'm just lucky, and things worked out right from the beginning. From the very beginning I was able to do what I wanted and also earn a living at it. And now with Party Packages, my commercial firm, doing so well, I really have no problems at all. Let me tell you what my latest gimmick is. I've made up a package of paper napkins, favors, hats, et cetera, for New Year's Eve celebrations, but the main feature is bibs. Bibs with nude male and female upper torsos painted on them. I can't keep up with the demand of department stores as far away as Austin, Texas. Seven years ago I had an idea—why not cushions to lean on that were effigies of mothers and other females. I did nothing with that idea. I was going through another kind of hell then, finding that I was no longer interested in the kind of painting I was doing—color field they call it now, as I've already mentioned—and wondering if I was all washed up. Or whether I even cared that I was all washed up. That question was even worse, to tell the truth. I felt I was dying, so I fiddled with some antiques which I had carted out of my mother's store (she has an antiques store) as a form of personal therapy. That was when I found out exactly what I wanted to do. I make these replicas, as you know, of rooms or parts of rooms and in some cases put in mannequins or dummies. These rooms are my art object. I'm entirely fulfilled in making these interior scenes. I really have no problems at all!" I exclaimed. "Designing for Party Packages leaves me plenty of time for my serious work. The fact is I'm just zooming along with both."

I certainly let the cat out of the bag there. I'd dug a perfect hole and fell right into it. I was the one who had said that my problem was the conflict between making my living at something I despised and trying to keep at my creative work.

Dr. Emerson said nothing. He knows how to wait. He knows how to bank his reactions and keep his thoughts to himself. He has fantastic self-control. He is terrific. (I want him to have a happy life. I hope everything works out all right for him.) After a patient leaves and before the next one arrives, I wonder if he kicks the furniture to let off steam. But nothing in his office looks damaged. Does he go to a gym at least once a week to slam at a punching bag? He's got to do something.

I felt like someone about to give himself up to the police because he couldn't stand the fear of betraying himself any longer. Emerson was probably dying for a cigarette, but he was committed to creating an atmosphere or a tension which would be broken if he did anything at all overt. I knew what he was up to, but I had got myself into this situation and my only recourse was to outwait him.

He didn't sigh or shift in his chair. The silence did not die—that is what really impressed me. The silence stayed alive. I wish with all my heart that circumstances were different. I feel that he and I could have become real friends. Our relationship would have been more mature than the one I have with Bob Meacham. But my analysis with him and my knowledge of his life—Emerson's—preclude our becoming the kind of friends I know we could be.

He won. Finally—it must have been ten minutes later by the clock —I said, "I can't think of a thing to say."

At once he asked, "After work, what is the most important thing in a man's life?"

After work? I thought. "Vacations?"

He laughed—a short bark, abruptly terminated. That remark did it. He lost his fantastic self-control that once. He was very upset he laughed. I guess he just couldn't help it. I can be very witty inadvertently.

Thereupon another long silence ensued. This time it was charged. Charged with his trying to recoup his loss—he had lost control there —charged with a certain meanness. I guess I'm saying I felt guilty, and so he seemed smug and even punitive. I felt like a mean bad boy.

After five minutes I said, "Love."

What could I do? I couldn't put it off any longer. I was human, after all.

Then he sighed. And the room seemed to rearrange itself. Nothing moved, but everything settled into place.

"Love is important too," he said simply. "Work *and* relationships."

I was overcome with sorrow. With weariness. With utter exhaustion. I wanted to draw sleep over me like a quilt and sleep it out, sleep out my despairing fatigue.

At the end of my rope, I said, "I'm in love. I'm sick with love, loving this girl who won't have anything to do with me. I think I might die."

I didn't look at him. I was talking to myself now. But I was aware he had turned his head just slightly, as though to avoid the full impact of what I was saying. He was listening with all his might at the same time. He was trying to see.

I didn't tell him anything else that time. I was too tired. I simply stated that Edith did not know anything at all. And that I did not want her to know anything at all. I looked at him. He returned my look. Of course, he is discreet. How discreet I did not fully appreciate then. But I had to say firmly, "My wife is never to know," to take care of my responsibility in the matter. I wasn't terribly nice in those days, but I wasn't all black.

"Sometimes I can't breathe," I said. "Naturally, I can't eat. I can't seem to swallow. It's been four months now."

I left, no longer a patient but an invalid. He saw me to the door as usual, but he thanked me that time. His thanks seemed remarkable and mysterious. Yes, he actually said, "Thank you," as I left.

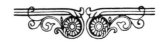

I went to bed for a day and a half after that. Edith brought me soup and bananas. I asked for the bananas. They go down easy and I know they're nourishing. I guess I really wanted to live, or would I have gone to Dr. Emerson in the first place?

"He doesn't seem to be doing you any good at all," Edith said, sitting on the edge of the bed.

"Leave me alone."

"You're worse instead of better. Why not try the other doctor?" She looked just like the girl I'd married seven years earlier. Her uncompromisingly straight dark blond hair was parted at the left side and the thick portion was tucked behind her right ear. It hung loose on the other side.

"Your ear never looks quite thawed out," I said.

"I'm serious!" she cried, sure of herself because she was on home territory. Other people's welfare, their interests, she will fight for tooth and nail. Her own are a different matter. Strange how my wife can't stand up for herself very well, like a dog who doesn't know that it is his own threshold that is to be defended, not the neighbor's. Except dogs are rarely mixed up in this regard. Only people are.

"Your ears always had a waxy look, like something out of Madame Tussaud's."

"You are *worse,*" she said hoarsely into my ear. "*Not* better. You've been going to this man for a month. Something is drastically wrong."

Edith is bright, very bright. I've always delighted in her brightness.

"Maybe—and this is *only* a suggestion—maybe you should try the other doctor," she said.

When I married her, she had a worried look too. A serious, worried, lovely face. I know I have been inconsistent. But she is lovely in this ordinary American beauty way. She has no idea she's quite beautiful. No one who knew she was beautiful would feel she had to read every liberal magazine published.

"It frightens me, you're so th-in-nn." She positively moaned.

"A bag of bones," I said, looking down my length. A man in bed is a ridiculous object. It gave me an idea I filed away in the back of my head. How about a scene called "The Bachelor" in which a large double bed, a girlie magazine, a darning egg and a torn pair of socks were featured? The whole thing would be seen from the top of the bed downward. The spectator himself would supply the head looking down on a skeleton complete except for the skull. To be alone, to be alienated, is like death. Without involvement, we are inert matter. That would be the idea. It was something to think about anyway.

"It's only been three weeks, six or seven sessions," I said. "I've got to give Emerson a fair chance."

The word "fair" was well chosen. Edith considers unfairness a cardinal sin. My girl's a good scout, and I know our daughter will grow up to be just like her lovely mother.

"Have another banana? I'll cut it up and put some heavy cream on it."

"No, I've got to sleep," I said. "You carry on as usual. I'm going to sleep until tomorrow afternoon."

"I've got to go pick up the daughter now." Amanda was at a neighbor's.

"I'll be all right, angel," I said. Edith is angelic in this liberal arts sort of way. Do I sound too impersonal? But I am a born observer.

"I love you," she said, her eyes filming up a bit.

I couldn't bring myself to return the compliment then. Given I wanted to pull the covers over me and daydream about Nan Weil, my conscience stood in the way. But I was hurting my wife, not saying anything. So I kissed her hand—two kisses. Europeans kiss hands just for *politesse,* so I was not being false technically. Only in every thought and breath I drew.

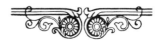

Seeing Emerson the next time, I felt sheepish, but you might say I was more relaxed. I came in my sneakers, suntans and checked shirt—what I wear at Party Packages. I had forgotten to change into regular shoes and a suit.

He noticed the difference; said nothing. I sat down, crossed my legs and started shaking my free foot. I was very aware of the sneakers in his office. As usual, I wore no socks—it gave me a resort sensation. White Protestant sports and easy camaraderie, look-ma-no-hands cycling, no strain, no sweat, some give and take, clam bakes, lawn mowing, the paper route, inadequate allowances, showing off, early betrayals, the wounded heart of a ten-year-old—all this I saw in my naked ankle.

"I used to wear moccasins at work," I said. "At Party Packages, that is. I do my other work at home. We have an extra bedroom; I work there and take part of the rent off income tax. I'm self-employed. It's deductible. I used to assemble the whole scene, but it's cumbersome. Now I just get the props together and submit a sketch. At home I still wear moccasins and real old clothes. When I'm being the artist, I have an image of myself to keep up as well, you know. It's double work—creating imagery in your work and keeping up an image of yourself. We artists are supposed to be bumpkins with straw in our hair, spewing tobacco and inarticulate philosophy. An unkempt guru mumbling against the conformity of the adjusted. Well, I can't quite maintain that posture, but I don't wash up or comb my hair before a visit from gallery or museum people. For my openings I always put on mismated pants and jackets and something in bad taste. The authentic is often gauche, so the atrocious is often taken for the authentic. Those who produce truthful, beautiful things are often at loggerheads with themselves and are tasteless. It's a paradox I roll with. I can manage to because I'm quite a relaxed person actually. At Party Packages I wear this outfit, except when it's cold and I put on a sweater. When department-store buyers come, I put on a suit and comb my hair. I don't wear it too long, do I?" I ran my shaking hand through my faded-looking hair. It has a tendency to lie like fern at the nape of my neck, and it is a little longer than the usual not-so-short American haircut. In England I'd look bookish; here I could pass for an architect, occupying a profession that mediates between ideal conception and the layman's pocketbook and plumbing requirements.

"You no longer wear moccasins at Party Packages?" Dr. Emerson asked.

"Sneakers are better," I said, "for clandestine activities," forcing myself to use the word, to face up to it. "I'm engaged in an illicit affair. If you ever saw her, you'd understand why. She's absolutely out of this world."

"I thought you said she'd have nothing to do with you."

I saw his point at once. "It'll be illicit the moment I can get to her. You're right. Strictly speaking, it can't be considered clandestine until I get near her."

"Does this . . . this woman live so far away then?"

"She's right above me!" I exclaimed, seemingly puzzled at his obtuseness. "Right above my head. Right on the floor above me, in the front office, right over where I design those damn aprons and tablecloths and serving trays. Right above my splitting head!"

The pump was at last primed. I began to talk of her, and Dr. Emerson no longer had to pull teeth. At least not for quite a while. The problem was not that I'd forgotten anything, I told him, but that I couldn't forget a thing. A case could be made that neurosis is having too good a memory but a buried one, I revised it to later. I tried to have a philosophical discussion with him about this on several occasions, but he gave me the impression that my interest itself was suspect, and he implied that I was wasting my money (he was quite conscientious about this) going into such theorizing, however interesting it might be. I suppose an analogy could be made with medicine: the doctor's business is to locate the tumor and treat it, not to discuss the intricate nature of fibrosis with the patient. But what if the patient is also engaged in a little laboratory work on the nature of being himself? Well, I couldn't budge him on this anyway. I couldn't understand then why he treated intellectualizing as a cardinal waste of time.

"I don't remember the first time I ever saw her," I told him. "All I know is that one day several months ago I saw her and knew I'd seen her before. I saw her and recognized her. I saw her for the first time, but with total recall. I saw her and she belonged to me. I saw her at the bus stop diagonally across the avenue. I was standing at my window, and there she was leaving the bus stop and jaywalking toward me. I felt a weakness down to my ankles. That bus stop is still killing me. I wish I could obliterate it, rub it out. Blast it to kingdom come. Damn bloody bus stop." I was sorry, but I couldn't help being emotional about it.

"She uses the same bus to come to work every day?"

"Every single day." The injustice of it all! "She must have been sick a couple of days last month. It should have been a relief, but I couldn't tear myself away from the window."

"It's not just doors then, it's also windows you're compulsive about."

I shook my head. "It's the door mostly. I'm surprised there isn't a rut in the floor by it. In seven years of marriage I've never looked at another woman. Is *that* my problem? But I'm simply not a philanderer. I'm not just chasing a skirt. If I thought I was just a two-bit skirt chaser, I'd blow my brains out." I had my pride even then! Or was I supposed to be embarrassed by my—what?—my inhibitions? my lack of initiative?

He seemed to nod impatiently; I got the idea he agreed with me and was eager that I get on with it. But—perhaps I *am* a hopeless puritan, deep and dyed. I had to make certain, absolutely certain, he did not think I was having a simple case of lust. "Do I look like a lecher?" I asked, spreading out my bony hands.

"You think it's a simple case of lust?" he asked, uncannily using my very own words.

"Of course not!"

So let's get on with it, he again seemed to suggest. But I couldn't let go until I was certain. "Do you?"

"That," he said, "is part of your problem." I suppose it was part of my problem too that I did not then and there ask him what the problem was. Would he have told me? No, it's up to the patient himself to find his way through the maze. So it's just as well I didn't ask him. (It wasn't till much later that it dawned on me what he was talking about.) At the time I thought he thought my problem was that I considered adultery sinful. His reaction opened vistas to me. Maybe psychoanalysis would make me a great lover. I started to laugh self-consciously.

He waited. Then I saw something else to laugh at and said, "Lechers don't lose twenty pounds over not sleeping with a girl."

He smiled.

I didn't say this to him then. But what had really made me seek out psychiatric help was this: I was puzzled, upset, frightened by the intensity of my passion for Nan Weil. I'd been married at twenty-nine, and I had had two or three relationships before that, which I'd conducted in my usual intense fashion. But this, this emotion which had appeared suddenly out of the blue, was something different in its direness.

Maybe, as Edith claimed, I was working too hard. Maybe what's been buried has to surface and like a whale sometimes comes up a long distance from its original appearance. I'm saying all this in a feeble attempt to justify what will appear like my unmitigated folly as I revealed it step by step to Dr. Emerson. But I was like an addict in need of a fix. Nan was my fix. Out of sight of her, I had withdrawal symptoms. These were the facts. Why would I pretend to or exaggerate such an ordeal of irrational emotion? I am sorry for the man that I was.

"I'm not as self-possessed as I seem to you," I said. He must have laughed privately over that for weeks, but he looked very solemn. "If I could possess her, I'd be all right. I'd be back to myself. I feel I'm not living in my body. I'm not in possession of myself. I'm halfway out of myself. I'm simply *not* myself."

While I was talking, he seemed, without actually stirring, to have moved to the edge of his seat. He was sitting on the edge of his seat. He was willing me to go on. To continue on this track.

"I've been reduced to such shamelessness. Or shamefulness. Which is it? It's sort of the same thing, isn't it? It's like the words 'regardless' and 'irregardless.' They sort of mean the same thing, don't they?" He was no longer sitting on the edge of his seat. "Why is being shameless so shameful?" He wouldn't give that possible subject of speculation elbow room; I was being too intellectual. Chastened, I returned to facts: "Sneakers don't make any sound. I can go to the door; and if Miss Price, my assistant, is bent over her work, she doesn't notice. I long for the sight of her."

"Miss Price?"

"God, no. Nan."

I am honorable. If he had had me drawn and quartered, I would not have told him her last name. I'd decided this even before my first session.

"She's married. I cannot tell you the rest of her name." If I'd not been so honorable, so strait-laced, there might have been no story to tell.

"Nan will do," he said. "It's not important what her last name is."

Oh poor man, poor Yale Herbert Emerson. In my analysis, often I didn't know what I was saying. Literally. But that he didn't know is too much. It's too much to bear. This cough of mine had not yet appeared, this cough which is the reason for my writing this down, out, up for myself to see, in a final summing up. I'm coughing it up, as they say.

"You can't go on referring to her as 'she' or 'her.' It's too confusing," he said. "Call her Nan."

"Nan passes my door on her way up or down four times a day. Sometimes more, if she runs out of something. Getting a glimpse of her is the only thing that's keeping me going.

"This is what I mean by shamelessness," I said, avoiding his eyes. I paused, embarrassed. "I go through her wastepaper basket. I mean, I go through her garbage. *I* go through her garbage." I leaned forward and pressed my head between my hands to crush out my humiliation. "I used to sneak upstairs every day after she'd left and go through the paper bag outside her door, which is usually a mess with butts and apple cores and sometimes the leavings of sandwiches. I don't do it any more. I really don't. But I used to. I did.

"These sneakers are very useful. They were a very good idea. I go downstairs to eat, and then I start up the stairs and sneak right by my door until I get to her landing. I pass the other two offices on her floor, and even if the doors are open no one notices me. I stand outside her door—it is always closed—and listen. It makes me feel better. If I hear her coming to the door, I can keep right on going up to the next flight. If, as has happened, Miss Price notices me halfway between our floor and the one above, I say I'm going to check the roof door. I make quite a thing about checking it in the heat to make sure it's opened so we get some cross ventilation. When it's really cold, I complain of drafts and rant about its not being hooked." I decided to bring it up. "I despise my own cunning. I'm very cunning. I feel my cleverness is very sick."

"It's an adaptation," he said. "You are simply adapting to your problem."

"But, if you cure me of my cleverness, I won't be an artist any more." I almost collapsed at the thought. "I won't be anything."

"I doubt that," he said very firmly.

"You do?"

"Yes. Cleverness, inventiveness, is not the question."

"Then what is!" I cried.

"*We* shall have to see," he said.

"Meaning I shall have to see!" I said resentfully.

Dr. Emerson is a man of few words professionally. And he did not choose to underline the obvious. But he was right unwittingly—he had to see too.

I was determined to be cured. Weeks went by and I told him everything. That was the idea, wasn't it? To keep nothing hidden. To reveal it all. Nothing was wrong with my memory. I kept trying to prove this to him. Having been one myself, I think A students are more perfectionists than they are naturally brilliant. My brilliance lies in other areas, in imaginative leaps, in associative connections. Not in the analysis of Carolingian history undertaken for a term paper. I kept telling him this. And telling him my love story at the same time. I did tell him all. Absolutely all. I was an A student.

"The first time I saw her must have been the second time," I told him, "for I was already hooked. She walks as if she's a little knock-kneed, though she has perfectly great legs, but women walk with that weird splaying out and coming together, as if the ball bearings need tightening. Her auburn hair is cut very short in a dedicated way, like someone who has taken vows to eliminate all fuss and bother. Like someone who has given herself over to a cause. Radical women, artistic and intellectual types affect this austerity. But from the neck down Nan is bourgeois. Beautifully bourgeois. I don't mean middle class. I mean womanly. Women are bourgeois; they superintend bourgeois virtues. It is their calling, or at least society has made it their calling: home, hearth, three meals a day, clean laundry, dusted book shelves, Kleenex in every bathroom, the safety and comfort of their husbands and children. Okay, Fem-Lib will string me up. Of course, women can be artists or anything else, too! But when things run smoothly, it is their doing. They are a private bureaucracy, tending the state of matrimony." Well, *he* had said I was inclined to be literary, so I let him champ at the bit.

"The nape of her neck is so vulnerable." I was in his office, sitting before some Danish teak, and the thought of the nape of her neck made me feel drained. It was as though some liquid, something my legs were filled with, was being drawn off into the floor. "A few days after the day I spotted her from the window—I'm telling you all— I looked up from my table at the delicatessen and I saw the nape of her neck. She was eating and reading a magazine at the same time. Every moment is precious to her. She's told me so.

"I got through my lunch before she did, so I had to walk by her to pay the cashier. I saw that she was reading *Antioch Review,* which interested me no end, of course. I remember wondering then if she had lunch there regularly. I was afraid to hope. That's what I'm here for," I cried incoherently, "to kill this hope."

"Why do you find hope so painful?"

"Hope is so hopeless."

I was very anxious. I caught on to that. I'd never known I was an anxious person. I'd lived with myself for thirty-six years when I said this to him, so how was I to know this person, me, could exist as the same person but also as a less anxious person. The anxiety I lived with was me, and I was used to that me.

"But she keeps giving me hope. Oh God, if she'd only stop."

"You are sure she gives you hope."

"I'm not in love with Ali MacGraw. I mean, this girl exists right over my head, she smiles at me, she's very kind. Not right away, she didn't smile at me right away, but now she does. She even wants one of the party packages I'm planning for the spring season. She said this to Miss Price. I think her kids could use one. She's giving me real encouragement."

It was winter then, and Dr. Emerson turned up the heat in the radiator, seeing I was shaking so. He took the opportunity to sigh, thinking I wouldn't notice. He sighed the moment his back was turned. He turned the switch. The sigh was over. He turned back and sat down.

"Later on, several days later, I was by the door unwrapping some cartons when I almost choked. I'm telling you everything—remember, this was only the third time I laid eyes on her. I saw her when she was two steps below my level. You see, for a split second I thought she was coming into my office. Maybe she's a buyer, I thought. In that split second I had time to imagine how I could take her out to several lunches before consummating the deal. But she continued up the stairs without even having noticed me. My heart labored like a marathon runner's.

"There are two one-man public relations offices in my building, one on the third floor, another on the fourth. There's an importer of watch straps, just the straps; there's a smalltime-nightclub booking agent, and so on. Some of them have full-time secretaries. Others use Manpower or Kelly Girl.

"She is so voluptuous and yet delicate. Her joints are fragile, and they make me weak. Her elbows, for instance (I had a good look at one of them as she went by), are so delicate you wouldn't think they'd hold the lower arm and the upper arm together for any length of time. Her arms are very rounded; her legs are straight and yet full, like a statue's; her behind is delicious. Altogether she's unbelievable."

At this point Emerson must have committed himself to a long haul.

"This girl is a foreign princess, I thought. Can she be working for watch straps? Life is too cruel! Her face is hard for me to describe. It's heady, like too much scent. That short hair makes her neck look almost too long for her proportions. Her nose is fine and a bit too long, her eyes are dark, her skin tone pale, her mouth clearly carved and yet soft. She is a beautiful Jewish girl, but that doesn't describe her at all. She makes Edith seem so two-dimensional, so recently made. Nan, on the other hand, looks as if a lot of history went into her, ages and ages of Mediterranean history, and she wears it like perfume." I was falling in love even more, telling him all this, I who thought I could fall no further.

"To the Anglo-Saxon," he said flatly, "Jewish, Italian, Greek types seem exotic."

"It's not that!" I protested. "It's Nan. I'm not in love with every Jewish girl walking by. A good thing too, since I live in New York." Emerson was white Protestant himself, I remember thinking. Did that mean he'd discount his attraction for, if he ever were attracted to, a Jewish girl in his own case? Discount his attraction for her automatically, because his attraction was too easily explained as being drawn to patent exoticism? There is no end to examining oneself and discounting one's inclinations. I mean, I did not marry Edith Shaw to prove I didn't find an Italian girl more attractive. Nor did I marry a Greek girl just to prove that I am not afraid to expose my interest in the exotic, as he calls it. There is nothing to be gained by this kind of cerebration. Nothing at all, and he would have agreed, but I didn't see that.

"I'm mad about her, and she happens to be Jewish. I'm sorry I mentioned the fact that she's Jewish."

"But why shouldn't she be Jewish?" he asked.

"But you just said—"

"I only meant that your description of her, your choice of adjectives, indicated that her exoticism may be a large factor in your feelings."

"But it's not. She's just a gorgeous female."

" 'A foreign princess'?"

"That's a figure of speech."

"Exactly. What does foreign mean to you?"

"Alien?"

"What else?"

"Foreign, just foreign." I didn't want to say "different, special," for then he'd have me again on the exotic bit. Anyway we were talking at cross purposes. Later on, however, I was to know what he was driving at.

"What I'm going to tell you now seems like low comedy. Like a cheap television serial, sort of pop life commenting on pop art. But at the very beginning I tried to create a couple of situations so I could officially meet her. I bought a roast beef sandwich, a take-out order of coffee and the best-looking cheese danish they had in the delicatessen, and then climbed the stairs to her floor. I had already found out she did something in the front office, which had no lettering on its door. Was she a private secretary to someone writing his memoirs, that kind of thing? I hadn't started going through her garbage yet. I knocked on the door. She came to it, opened it, small, wide-eyed, blinking a little. She'd chewed off her lipstick and consequently looked younger than I remembered, like a wife before breakfast.

"I looked down at her and found I couldn't speak my set piece. I handed her the paper bag. She took it before she realized she had anything in her hand. She must have been deep in her work before I knocked. When she realized she'd taken it, she almost dropped it, as if it were a time bomb.

" 'Your lunch,' I said. She's inclined to be absent-minded, just like me, I thought, when she said, 'Did I order anything?' as if to herself.

" 'I'm George Safford downstairs,' I said. 'I'm Party Packages. They delivered this to me, but I figured it must be for you. I'm so glad to be meeting you at last.'

" 'I never eat at Party Packages,' she said. 'I mean I never order from there. I bring my own lunch or go downstairs. But what am I telling you all this for?' She handed me the package and backed into the room. She was about to close the door.

"I suppose I looked desperate. She is kind, no question about it. She said, 'Try next door. Maybe it's their lunch,' and closed the door and locked it from inside."

I told Emerson I had the clear impression she didn't see me. The way you don't really see the waiter who serves you or know what the driver of the bus you're on looks like. (Bob Meacham, I suspect, she sees clearly enough. Oh God!)

I'd had another idea, which I also told Dr. Emerson about in detail. Having just finished a children's party package, replete with space platforms, I decided to throw a party before I cleared out my free-lance assistants and the wreckage a big job always left. I invited everyone in the building. On the invitation I pushed under her door, I simply typed, "Celebration cocktails, George Safford, second floor. Everyone invited Thursday at five." I did not write Party Packages, since she seemed under the impression it was a short-order caterer. I added, in my handwriting and as a casual afterthought, "Safford is a well-known artist, represented at the Guggenheim."

Everybody turned up but her, and they drank up everything. I was no good at inventing situations. I kicked myself for not having written R.S.V.P. But I wasn't thinking clearly, though I was thinking too much.

Then one day fate intervened. She was going down to the delicatessen just as I was leaving with some things for the post office. In my fright or anguish I dropped the three rolls wrapped in brown paper and the two parcels, which went bouncing down the stairs. She cried out (women are jumpy) and then began to help me pick them up. I saw, my heart leaping with joy, that she was, indeed, a very kind person. She handed me a couple of items and proceeded down the stairs ahead of me.

This was my chance and I didn't muff it. "You didn't come to the party," I said.

She tried to look back without losing her balance. "Oh. No. I . . . I couldn't make it." But I could tell she'd had no intention of making it. "You gave the party?" We were standing face to face on the sidewalk.

"I'm George Safford," I said, unable to extend my hand.

She acknowledged me by nodding her head slightly, full of a simple wariness but not wishing to be rude. "Hi."

She turned into the delicatessen. I followed her in. We took a table for four so I had chairs on which to put my parcels. It was as easy as that, that first time I had lunch with her. I couldn't get over the ease. I can't remember a thing she said. I don't think she said anything, though she told me her name. I remember telling her all about Party Packages and how I'd started it three years before. Then I think it suddenly dawned on her she was lunching with a strange man. Over ice cream she excused herself matter-of-factly and opened up the magazine she had with her. She read the *Atlantic* placidly while I simply drank in her presence. Since I'm realistic, I didn't feel insulted or anything. There was nothing to feel insulted about. She hadn't counted on having lunch with me or anyone else.

One day something traumatic happened. I was standing outside her door when she opened it and stepped out. She looked startled but not frightened. I froze to the spot, speechless. "What's the matter?" she asked.

"I've been glued to your door," I answered, dying at the sound of my words.

She laughed. She didn't believe me, so I lost nothing by that incident. In fact, I believed I profited from it in the long run. They say, "Get a married woman to laugh, and she's half yours."

Ostentatiously I climbed up toward the roof door. When I got back down and looked through the delicatessen window, she was ordering her lunch. I joined her.

"I'm glad you keep checking that roof door," she said. "Anyone could come down from some other building. I'm thinking of putting a peephole in my door."

"I can do that for you," I said at once.

"I can get a man up."

"I put in my own. There's nothing to it."

She didn't commit herself to anything and went back to reading the *Paris Review*.

"Are you a literary agent?" I asked her, just as an opener.

"I really don't have time to talk," she said. "Every moment is precious to me." That was the first time she said anything to indicate time was on her mind a lot. I began to notice more of this later on.

Dr. Emerson was with me as I told him all this, but he wasn't listening hard. I was, however, actually benefiting from my confession. It was good to tell someone all about Nan. Because I had to keep my affair from Edith, I was, in a sense, only half facing it myself. Telling Dr. Emerson made me feel I had at least not dreamed it all up. Better an agony that was real than a sense of doubt about its actual existence. I have always had a real drive for health.

"That was when I got it bad," I said, realizing it for the first time. I looked at him with some surprise.

"Got what bad?"

"I was wrong, it was inaccurate to say I was hooked that time I saw her at the bus stop. I was hooked, it's true. But only with passion, you might say. After she said, in that rather pedantic tone of voice, 'I really don't have time to talk,' I began to feel fearful. That's the only word for it."

"Anxious," he said.

"Scared, scared somehow she was already slipping away."

"You felt abandoned?"

"I felt the beginning of this nausea."

"Good." He meant, Good, maybe we're getting down to brass tacks.

"You were hooked now—not with passion, but with what?"

"She's so womanly and so cool. So God-awful cool."

"She was so self-sufficient?"

I don't think so any more, but then I said, "She's so cool, so perfect."

"She seemed so self-sufficient?" he insisted.

"Yes." I've had moments in my analysis when I've felt ornery. This exchange with Dr. Emerson put my back up. I was glad my back was up; somehow it seemed as if something was taking. I wasn't going in for finicky nonsense, and I wanted him to know it. I felt pretty sure of myself. I thought.

"In relation to her, you felt . . . ?"

"Awful." I liked the non-analytic simplicity of that word.

"Good," he said. "You felt a lack of self-sufficiency?"

"I'm quite self-possessed," I said. "From the earliest time, I've relied on myself, made my own way. I worked through college, and

I knew what I wanted to do. By the way, when I told you earlier I had my first one-man show at twenty-three, I did not mean here in New York. It's a good thing too. I was in my abstract expressionist stage then. I had the show out on Long Island, sold the whole thing out, but it didn't count against me when my style changed. It was while I was doing color field that I showed here at the Conreid, which is a first-rate gallery."

"You relied on yourself from the earliest time," Dr. Emerson said, plowing his way ruthlessly through all of that irrelevant information. "Isn't that unusual?"

"I'm an all-round self-reliant American boy. No one can take that away from me."

"Did you live on Long Island as a boy?"

"Summers we lived on Long Island. Winters we lived near Pough-keepsie. My father was a general practitioner, a small-town doctor."

"He is no longer?"

"He died when I was, let's see, twenty-five. He dropped dead from overwork, in my opinion."

Dr. Emerson looked terribly interested. I laughed. In his usual fashion, he let me laugh.

"I'm laughing because there's nothing in my background at all. Nothing peculiar for us to poke into. It was a perfectly normal back-ground. My father didn't die when I was two. I was twenty-five. I had an absolutely typical American childhood, beaches, school, camps, et cetera, et cetera."

" 'The Porch' at the Guggenheim," he said, "has something to do with beaches, summers."

He has a retentive memory. It was more than two months since he'd seen my scene, but he obviously remembered the sand sifting.

"If I remember correctly," he said, "the first time you told me of your work, you said you used dummies in your scenes."

"Sometimes. A figure or two. It depends." Then I told him of the idea I had for "The Bachelor." I had already put in an order with my mother for an old brass bed. "Next time she goes to one of her antiques auctions, she'll let me know if she sees a likely piece of furniture. I'll pay anything for it. It's got to be a double bed."

"There is no one on your porch," he remarked. He was really seeing.

I shrugged. "That could be the whole point," I said.

"I think so too."

"I intended a lonely mood. A lonely waiting, so I left out persons."

"You left out a person."

"Yeah, there's no one there," I said, thinking of Nan. I still did not know what she did above my head. I sent her a flower. Not a real one. I made a flower of cardboard and foil, gold foil, which went with her auburn hair, and had a messenger service I used take it to her. I suppose they thought it strange getting a small package to deliver one flight up in the same building. But I tip well.

That afternoon there was a knock on my door. The door was partially open as usual, but someone was knocking on the frame. I went to it. Miss Price was doing bookkeeping by the window. Nan stood outside with the flower in her hand, which she thrust at me.

"I am a married woman," she said. "Happily married. I don't want to encourage you, so here, I'm returning it right away. I have no time for hanky-panky." She turned, her face flushed.

Just before starting up the stairs, she said, "Nor the inclination."

Her eyes shone. I thought she really saw me for the first time, and I didn't get the impression she hated me. She was annoyed, but she didn't dislike me. On such crumbs did my life depend.

"You see," I told Dr. Emerson, "she gave me something to go on. I'm not in love with someone on the moon. She said, 'Nor the inclination,' when she could have left it at 'I have no time for hanky-panky.' Her saying 'Nor the inclination' proves she had considered it—me— or she wouldn't have got to the point of wondering if she did or did not have the inclination to have an affair. I could write dialogue for a play and drop significant clues foreshadowing what is to come." Dr.

Emerson was not impressed, though I turned out to be right later, quite a while later. He consistently refused to be impressed with my powers of ratiocination.

Miss Price said, "Well!" when Nan left me with the flower in my hand. I don't know what she overheard. The sound of traffic at the window can obliterate conversations at the other end of my office, which is over sixty feet long. She, Miss Price, did not know the flower was of my own making or that it had been delivered to the gal upstairs. Maybe she thought Nan was bold and on the make. It just shows how you can't be sure of appearances. I would not like to be a witness in court. I'd make a poor one and a worse juror. I see too many possible possibilities. And I always concede to every possible possibility. I do honor ambiguities.

Two weeks later Miss Price, looking excited, told me, "She was here again, and left this memo pad behind with her phone number printed on it!"

"Who?"

"The mother of three upstairs."

My stomach pitched over. Damn it, she had been here, and I had to be out to lunch. "Mother of three?"

"That's what she said."

"Why?"

"How should I know?"

"I mean why did she come here?"

"She needed to staple something together. She writes."

"She writes!"

"That's what I said. She said she was sending out some material. That's exactly what she said. It looked like poetry to me."

"She's a poet!"

"I bet she's just a professional typist by the hour."

"With an office all her own?"

"Maybe she is a poet," Miss Price said with a snort. "In this city you meet all sorts. She can afford an office but she can't buy herself a stapler. How do you like that!"

My heart expanded until I thought it would be torn apart. A poet. In my high school days I was in love with the writers I read, because they saw. They understood humanness, so they spoke directly to me. I felt reprieved. This girl might hold me off as a woman, but as a poet she would know what I was going through. Again I felt I had been given something more to go on. It was then that I began to go through her garbage bags. And understood what some of those tattered sentences on scraps of torn paper were.

It was then that I betrayed my condition by going to the door when Bob Meacham was around to notice. By then I was shaking and emaciated. I had known her four months. She'd barely noticed me, but I did not think she disliked what little she'd noticed. It was now several months later, and Dr. Emerson was a part of my life, a lot bigger part than Nan was. As I've said, I was addicted; *I* was nothing but a craving.

The intensity of my anguish lived a life of its own; Nan was above my head every day, but in all those months, including staring at the nape of her neck in the delicatessen the first time, I'd been actually near her about thirty non-consecutive minutes.

Just because someone is seeing a psychiatrist does not mean life around him stops. No, life has a way of going on. It has to. That's just the way it is. Reality is real.

Edith, my wife, was coming to an important decision, one in which my cooperation was essential. Puttykins, our daughter, is now three and a half. At the time I am writing about, Amanda was going on two and a half. Edith is not a demanding person, which, as I've said, is her problem; and while I was a bag of skin and bones, she didn't ask me to perform my duties as a lover. She's generous and she never let it be felt that she was neglected. None of that inverted martyrdom act: I am being brave, but not so brave that you fail to notice I'm being brave. Edith is too direct for this, too honest, too unspoiled. While I was really ailing, Edith left me alone. Of course, I was in too selfish a state even to appreciate it. But after all, she is young, healthy and quite passionate. She is not courageous when it comes to asking something for herself. I suppose, now that my appetite was returning somewhat (just seeing Dr. Emerson, even though I hadn't got to the root of the matter, ameliorated the worst of my physical symptoms), and I shook only at work, Edith had been waiting for me, had been hoping I would make love to her again. As usual, she put off speaking up for herself until she'd built up a head of despair. I woke up one night to find her crying.

At once, since I'm intuitive, I knew why. It's not good to be too intuitive; you in effect beat the other person to it—you accuse yourself even before he can. I felt guilty, too guilty to touch her. Too guilty even to comfort her.

She had sat up in bed and was noiselessly blowing into Kleenex. Even in this exigency she didn't want to disturb me. After crying for a while, she always sits up, I suppose because it's harder to breathe through a stuffed nose lying down.

The despair she builds up to makes her able to be angry. As I have said before, she can't get angry easily over wrongs done to her personally, only to me or Amanda or to anonymous peasants in war-torn countries.

When she saw I was awake anyway, she cried out, "You don't care for me at all! I'm just the housekeeper you happen to sleep next to!"

"That's not true."

"You haven't touched me in months!"

"I haven't been up to it," I said, which was a fact. I had not had a surplus of physical energy. I longed to touch her now.

"Your damn analysis is turning you into a cold fish."

I hope so, I thought. That would take care of everything.

"I hate Emerson!" she cried, in double despair now because she knew she was being irrational. Edith believes wholeheartedly in the virtues of reason, in being judicious, fair, above prejudices and spite. She buried her head in the pillow.

With a jerk she sat up to gasp for air. "But I hate myself even more."

She had no reason to hate herself, none whatsoever. I was certainly making a mess of everything to bring her to this.

"Why should you hate yourself?"

"Because I'm apparently unattractive, unwanted . . ." She broke into racking sobs.

It was either my integrity or her unhappiness. I put my arm around her and buried my face in her neck. I almost said, the idea having suddenly come to me, Why don't you go to bed with Bob Meacham. It might do you some good. I thought, I must tell Emerson this. It seemed to be the measure of my madness. I, the Calvinist, not only longed to be in someone else's sheets, I wanted my wife to sleep with my best friend. This has got to stop, I vowed, and started to shake in earnest. I shook so hard even her body vibrated.

Edith gradually stopped crying. She did not soften toward me too quickly. She has her pride, her diffident pride, to worry about too.

"Do *you* think Emerson is doing you some good?"

"It takes time. It's some kind of deep-seated business. He knows what he's doing."

"But you've got to feel that," she said, for she's not stupid. "If you don't feel that, you're resisting; if you do, you're his patient forever. He can't lose."

"I do love you or I wouldn't be going to him in the first place," I said.

I suppose that hadn't ever occurred to her. It was the first time it had occurred to me.

"I don't mind if we have less to live on. You know that," she said. "I always have said give up Party Packages if it bothers you. It's too crass. You're an artist." Of course, that's what she thought I was talking to Emerson about.

I kissed her neck as disinterestedly as possible, but responsive as always, Edith flung her arms around me. One thing led to another in the usual order. We made love for the first time in several months. Why go in for the usual details? Typically, with Edith it was very good. Afterward she said, "I've been thinking. If we're going to have another baby, this is the time to start trying. By the time I get

47

pregnant"—it had taken over a year the first time—"and the nine months are over, Amanda will be going on five. That's already too big a difference in age."

Her face, still a little swollen, was wreathed in expectations. "I'll have to unearth that thermometer again," she said. We'd been through months of temperature taking, catching the rise in her temperature, which indicated ovulation, to make love, whether it was two-thirty in the afternoon when she'd call me home from work or in the midst of doing the dinner dishes.

I tried not to *be*. Just not to be anything. Not myself; not her husband; not, just not. If I was nobody, I would not be lying here longing for Nan, hating myself for taking my wife when my heart wasn't in it, dreading making another new life simply by an act of my body. If I were not, I would not be a stranger threatening my own life.

I really *saw* that night how being "out of oneself," being unintegrated, could cost one one's life. I could ruin my marriage, bring a half-wanted person into the world on the wreckage of that very marriage, destroy my business, for I was killing my health simply because of my emotions. What *were* these emotions?

I was face to face with possible catastrophe. The destructiveness was in me. In me alone.

"I'm really scared," I told Dr. Emerson. "I've got to keep at this thing and really get it all cleared up. Nan smiled at me the other day, I'll have you know. She looked at me and smiled. I really feel she has some feeling for me."

"You've been coming here three, four months now and you still haven't told me about your family," Emerson said between ruefulness and disgust.

He was giving me that special look of his—alert, dispassionate, neutral, almost melancholy. Or was the melancholia I thought I saw simply an aspect of my own? At first, the more I grew to know the more melancholy I became. Thinking can make one melancholy. Perhaps that's why few people choose to think. But melancholia is easier to bear than despair. And when I knew less, I was in despair. Melancholia comes after you have awakened from sleepwalking, as despair is the desperate struggle to remain asleep, for to wake is possibly to die. Yet the choice is either to sleep over the abyss and possibly fall in unknowing, or to open one's eyes and possibly suffer the terror of being unable to keep oneself from falling anyway. But I'm being pedantic and running ahead of my story and informing it with hindsight. I was as melancholy then as I am free and excited now.

"Did you ever have a family?" he asked flatly.

"I have one daughter and a wife. A cleaning woman comes twice a week. *They're* all right. It's *me, me!* Why waste time talking about them?"

"Sometimes I think you're an orphan," he said, with great wisdom, I might add.

"But I'm not," I said. "My mother lives in the Village, where she has this antiques store. We see her regularly. She's no problem at all. In fact, if it weren't for hauling some of her junk, I would never have got the idea for my scenes. There's nothing wrong there really. Nan seemed very happy the last time I met her on the stairs. She looked like the cat who'd swallowed the canary. Her face was transfigured with happiness."

"Any time you want me to put in the peephole for you is fine," I said to her. "Let me do a little something for you."

"Are you like this with everybody?" she asked.

That is the problem courtship presents—the early phases of it. The man always runs the danger that the girl may think he behaves importunately with everyone, anyone.

"Do I look like a"—I hesitated—"a roué?"

"What a dated word!" She smiled at it—the word. She's interested in words.

All this on the stairs, one foot higher than the other, waiting for her to make room for me on the narrow landing. Why did I say it!

God, I wasn't thinking clearly. "I'm a married man," I declared. "With a daughter."

She looked alarmed for the first time. "And I have three children," she flung back, continuing up the stairs.

"I know," I cried out. "Miss Price told me."

But I was getting a reaction out of her; I was making contact. I kept pointing it out to Dr. Emerson. This whole thing was not in my head alone. But even if it were, does that put its reality in doubt? The person who thinks he's in love, acts on it, gets married, produces children on the strength of this illusion, if indeed it is an illusion. I felt good talking to her; even the paucity of our exchanges felt good. That's all I can say. I, the old George Safford, felt good. (I can hardly believe it now.) I enjoyed talking to her. Alive, anxious and dying.

"I worship the ground she walks on," I told Emerson. I was a walking cliché, but I couldn't help it. This thing was bigger than I. Another cliché.

"Ground," he said. "What does 'ground' mean to you?"

There he goes again, I thought. What does 'foreign' mean? Foreign means alien, different, exotic.

"Earth."

"You worship the ground she walks on. What do *you* walk on?"

"Thin air," I answered, off the top of my head.

"So it is the ground she walks on you worship. Not her."

As Edith put it, I had to believe he knew what he was doing. So I tried, against my better judgment, to keep up my end of this exchange. "I'm not mad for the country. But anyway, the earth here, I mean, the ground here in the city isn't earth. It's cement, asphalt, wood, who knows what." I really didn't see.

"What else does the word 'ground' bring to mind?"

I simply couldn't follow his train of thought.

"What does 'to hold your ground' mean?"

"To . . . to guard your place, your position."

"Do you have any place in the scheme of things?"

"I have a place in life!" I exclaimed. "I'm a successful man, holding my own."

"Good," he said. "What does 'holding your own' mean?"

"Sticking up for yourself. Making sure you aren't losing out."

"Good." He seemed quite excited. "What does 'own' mean?"

"Your own, my own, her own. I have no place at all in her life," I wailed. "I am groundless."

He let me go that day without any further torture.

I am groundless. The more I thought about it, the less sense the three words made. An accusation could be groundless, but not a person. To be grounded meant to be firmly planted, confirmed, based in fact and reason.

He was off on another tack the next time. "You're not mad for the country, as you put it."

"I'm the urban type. I like diversity, stimulation, juxtapositions, action, lights."

"You spent many summers in the country as a child?"

"I had my fill. But Edith and I are planning to build out in the Hamptons in a year or two. With children, you have to have a country place; it's not fair to them not to." Then I told him we had begun to try to have a second child. I told him how I felt about making love to Edith. I simply left myself out of it. Her husband made love to her, not I, George P. Safford. I could tell he did not find this solution to a difficult problem a strange one for me to have evolved.

"I have it in me to wreck the lives of several people," I said. "One mad passion and all can be lost."

"A passion you can count on being frustrated will lose you nothing," he said cryptically.

"She's coming around," I retorted. "I'm a perceptive person. I can tell I'm making a dent in her."

"After six months of longing you haven't even had a cup of coffee with this woman."

"Oh yes I have. I had lunch with her less than four months ago."

"Because you happened to walk into the delicatessen at the same time. But you haven't even invited her out for a cup of coffee, and she hasn't accepted an invitation from you."

"You mean I'm taking crumbs and making a whole loaf out of them."

He waited.

"But she's married, has children. Why should she be an easy mark?"

"Go on."

"She's extremely mature. She's behaving very responsibly. She is sure of herself as a woman. She doesn't need to be reassured."

"Yes, yes."

"She doesn't need me. It's me who needs her. I *am* realistic enough to see that. I'm not given to fantasies." Oh yes, yes. I said to Emerson, "I'm not given to fantasies." I, the metaphor maker, the artist. It was he who had really seen "The Porch."

But he helped me face up to one thing that day: I was taking crumbs. As a result of this recognition, my pride learned it was injured. I was determined to have at least a slice, one thin slice of bread. After all, I did have her phone number on the memo pad she'd left behind.

I telephoned her. While Miss Price was out of the office, I wiped my wet palms, picked up the telephone and dialed her number. I am George P. Safford, I said to myself. I have something in the permanent collection at the Guggenheim. I have a growing reputation in Boston and Chicago, and a new commission is pending. I am going to be a rich man someday because of Party Packages. If you, Nan, reject me, I still have Edith and Amanda to fall back on. (God, how callous I sound to myself now.) Thus I encouraged myself as I was dialing, my head all pulse, beating its surreal chimes.

"Hello, darling," she said, answering on the first ring.

I must have dialed wrong. "Nan?" My voice was hoarse. My heart floated.

She seemed to gasp. "Who's that!"

"George Safford."

"I thought you were my husband," she said. "Only my husband ever calls me here. What do you want?"

"I have a book of poetry I'd like to give you over a cup of coffee downstairs."

She sighed extravagantly.

Suddenly I felt waggish. "I'm married; you're married. I'm not up to anything really. I'm simply an ardent admirer from afar." I really sounded sophisticated, which didn't bother me at all.

"I'm working."

"I have a poet friend, Bob Meacham. He's a serious poet," I said. "I want you to know I'm interested in poetry."

"How do you know I write—poetry?"

"Miss Price told me, my assistant." I did not quote a line I'd found among apple cores: "In time, it is time consumes us all."

"I've heard of Meacham," she said. "Didn't he have something in the *Paris Review* recently?"

I didn't know, but I said, "He's a heavy contributor." I used Bob Meacham as a Good Housekeeping seal—it made me more kosher, as we say in New York. I thought it was very clever of me to use Bob Meacham. I did this deed to myself.

"Whose book is it you want to give me?"

"Catherine Emmerich. She's very good. My wife thinks she's going to develop into a major poet. My wife has very good taste. She majored in English lit."

"Well, I could do with a cup of coffee," she said. "But just fifteen minutes. I've no time to spare." She certainly had a thing about time, I noted.

It amazes me how canny one can be under pressure. I was practically blind (sic!) with joy, sitting down with her over a cup of coffee (she had accepted an invitation from me! She was looking at a book I'd purchased for her!), blind, yet not unseeing. She was overdue for a haircut (and indeed the next day she had one), so that she had constantly to brush some lengths of hair out of her eyes. Every time she did, her diamond ring flashed, proclaiming she belonged to someone else. She wore a kind of French wool T-shirt and culottes—most women look awful in culottes but not her. She had no lipstick on that day at all, just eye makeup, emphasizing the thickness and the straightness of her lashes. The straightness of her lashes cuts the corners of her eyes in such a way they seem almost square at the outside corners. They are big and thoughtful and interior-oriented. I always have had the feeling she takes me in in relationship to what she's actually considering within herself at the time. Thus, she could look directly at me, at a man, and not seem to be coy, to be asking for any sort of sexual response. She has this disinterested and yet utterly personal way about her. Nan never grinds any sort of ax, like, I'm beautiful or I'm an intellectual. She's entirely herself, which is why, as I explained to Dr. Emerson, she seemed self-possessed, sure of herself. (However, I am no longer certain of this.)

As I've said, I was canny. To make her feel safer, I spoke of Edith and Puttykins all during coffee. Nan listened; she said something about how busy her life was, squeezing in her work with running a home, maintaining a busy social life for her husband and herself, et cetera. She had her own office here to get away from the racket of three little ones at home, of course. She seemed less wary of me than ever before. The book of poetry, she commented, after lifting up the jacket to examine the binding, "is well made." Most people don't have any interest in the way a book is made. I fell even more in love with her, if that was possible. "If Stevenson says she's good, she must have something," she said, reading a quotation from the critic which was printed on the back of the jacket. "Thank you," she said, accepting the book. "Now I must get back to work." And so she ended our first coffee klatsch.

"What do you write about? Who do you write like?" I asked as we climbed the stairs. Stupid, unanswerable questions, but I wanted to prolong our stay together.

"I write poetry. Just poetry," she said and climbed away from me.

"That's really all I write." A funny thing to maintain so insistently: poetry was all she wrote. I failed even to see that I found her insistence peculiar.

I felt I'd got further in my relationship with her, yet, as I pointed out to Dr. Emerson, I was even more depressed the next two weeks. This, for some reason, did not surprise him. I remember thinking he had the qualities of a warlock, a male witch. He was somewhat occult, looking out of those dilating eyes, always urging me on.

"Describe what being in love feels like."

I went into my feelings of excitement and deprivation halfheartedly. Being in love was a subject that everyone knew about. What on earth could I contribute to its description? I said I felt it was like being saved from myself. Like being rescued. Or, conversely, like dreading not being rescued.

"That is the way it feels to you," he said.

"Of course, to me."

He waited.

"You mean that is not the way it feels to other people? I don't believe it!"

"When you were in love with your wife, before you were married, how did you feel?"

"Before I married her, or after I married her?"

"Both."

"Before I married her, at the beginning, I felt desperate. Yes." I was disheartened to see I'd had the same feelings then too. "I felt desperate until I suddenly realized she was desperate to marry me. In fact, I almost didn't marry her because of that. I mean the passion was out of it. I was sure of getting her."

"When you weren't sure, you were more passionate?"

"That's normal, isn't it?"

"Why did you marry her anyway, given you felt a letdown in your feelings about her?"

Now I understood why analysis was supposed to be rather hard on the patient's spouse. The patient's spouse usually felt left out or threatened or even somewhat paranoid. I'd gathered this from clues dropped by friends who'd been in analysis. I myself now felt I was betraying Edith, talking about my own motivations so honestly. What had she married, anyway—someone whose motivation had been less than pure, strong, outgoing love? This added to my guilt feelings toward her, something I had not expected from my treatment.

"I married her because I could no longer take being dangled or what-have-you by all those other women. She really wanted me, so I thought I'd settle for less passion and more quiet affection and security." I hated myself for letting him get this out of me. I sounded so—so cold-blooded.

"Well, that's not the whole story," I corrected myself. "I'm being too hard on myself."

"I think so too," he said.

"There were a couple of girls somewhere in there a couple of years before I settled down who really wanted me. But I didn't want them. I was barely attracted, to tell the truth, but I tried, I worked at, being more attracted to them. I said to myself, This girl or that other girl is willing to lead any kind of life I lead. Am I uninterested in her simply because she's nice to me? You see," I pointed out to Emerson with a hint of pride, "I was onto certain things about myself, but none of this applies to the Nan business. I finally figured out that just because someone was interested in me was no reason in itself to make myself like her. Now that *is* sensible. I can't believe that isn't sensible. But Edith came along and I *was* attracted to her, really desperately at first, as I said, and then I found out she wanted to marry me, so I didn't let that let-down feeling stand in the way. So I married her. And they lived happily ever after." I laughed.

"*I* have no doubt you love Edith," he said. "But you doubt you love Edith."

"What did I say to indicate that?"

"Love to you is despair," he said.

"Then love to Edith is despair too."

"But you're my patient here, not Edith."

"Edith was desperate to marry me. If I didn't call her up four times a day toward the end of our courtship, she thought I'd changed my mind. She's quite unsure of herself," I said. "It's amazing how unsure of herself she is. Her unsureness is a deep-seated thing going back to her childhood."

"Yes?" he said, as if asking a question. *Childhood?* he said. "We're analyzing you, not Edith."

"I realize that," I said. "It really is amazing how unsure of herself she is. But women have it over us. When they get anxious, as she used to get when I happened to miss my regular hours for phoning her, she could weep a bit and get rid of the tension. We men have to hold it in."

"Repressing one's feelings can lead to physical maladies as well as emotional ones," he said, leading me on.

"Edith can be so didactic, so sure—that's the only word—about something like corruption in the government or unfairness to minorities, and yet practically fall apart when I say, 'Your hair looks ratty today.' She has no defenses for something like that."

"If love equals despair to you, what, in this equation, does despair equal?"

"If x equals y, y has to equal x," I said quickly, the A student.

"In other words . . . ?"

"Despair equals love," I said.

"To you," he said, "despair equals love."

"To me?" I said, still not getting it in all its implications.

"To you." He looked straight into my eyes. "Do you see what I mean?"

That's all we had time for that session.

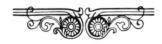

"Replica" is not the correct word for the kind of object I make. A replica is a copy, a facsimile of the real. A painting of a vase is a copy of the real vase, say, yet it is not a replica. It is something in itself: a painting.

My porch at the Guggenheim is not a replica of a porch, though it is an artful façade which looks like a porch and which, if you really wanted to, you could step onto and sit down in. It is not a copy. It's a number of objects assembled to look like a real porch. In a sense it is as real as a real porch—since you can walk onto it and even peer into the windows. My kind of art is real in a double way: it both looks like the real thing and, because of its size and three-dimensionality, *is* a real thing. It is not just appearances, in the way that a bit of grease on a canvas appears like flesh on a Renoir girl's arm. Though my scenes are more real than this, they are also simply appearances. Sometimes I think that word would be a good name for the kind of thing I do. Three-dimensional appearances. My work is not happenings, which exist only as they are happening and die right afterward. Mine are permanent dreams for waking eyes to see.

Or, to put it another way, my work is reproductions which attempt to reproduce the atmosphere of the original but which are originals in themselves. What I select to reproduce and the way in which I manage to produce the effect I desire on the spectator is wherein I am an artist. As Emerson so correctly put it, I am somewhat literary in my orientation. I go for stories rather than just visual sensations. But I tell a story visually. I exhibit a metaphor visually.

A display of living-room furniture at Sloane's reproduces a living room, but not a living room in which people have spent their lives. My reproductions always suggest that people have been there, may still be there, or are just about to return. Every object has been saturated with human history. It isn't easy to do, believe me. Dredging up my unconscious, objectifying it consciously so that it will tap the unconscious understanding of other people, is quite a tall order. In his way, Emerson was trying to make me dredge up something so that I, the dredger and the dredged, could see it for what it was. This too is a tall order. I admire the man very much.

"I'm no Don Juan," I told him, "but I like girls."

"That's good," he said.

"But by the standards and practices of the younger generation, I was very backward." I realized I was abashed at my retardedness. "I didn't really set my sights on a girl until college. These days kids are going steady at twelve. But I didn't start thinking about a girl until late, when I was seventeen. That is late, isn't it? I was terribly naïve. I'd been much too busy taking care of myself up till then to think about frivolous things like dating."

"Taking care of yourself?" he asked eagerly.

"I've already gone into that. I told you I was the self-reliant all-round American kid."

"What did this self-reliance consist of?"

"Mowing lawns, doing construction work for an architect friend of my parents, being a camp counselor, and so on. The girl I set my sights for in college was a year ahead of me. I guess she liked younger men." I found my remark delightful and took time to savor it. Emerson waited.

"I was seventeen, she was eighteen, so I guess she must have liked men who were a lot younger."

He smiled grudgingly. Dr. Emerson's goal is to get at what's bothering people and keeping them from functioning in society or from living up to their own full potential. He hopes to cure them of blocks, psychosomatic illnesses, destructive, unrealistic drives, or crippling fears. He looks into the human abyss every hour and succeeds in dragging some people out of it. You would think that anyone so involved with human anguish and possible tragedy would allow himself a little leeway, a little self-indulgence when he could. But he is a strict self-disciplinarian. He never smiled when a smile might hurt my feelings. He never smiled when he found me ridiculous, as I often found myself. He never sighed so I could know it. Or rather, when he sighed openly, I knew it was a hint that I was dwelling on something unnecessarily long. He never lighted a cigarette when to light it might break the necessary therapeutic tension, so that when he lighted it, I knew we were just poking around and not really digging. He never fidgeted unless to fidget was part of the treatment.

At least this is how it all appeared to me. I've said before I can't be sure of remembering everything exactly. But the way things appear to one is how you must take them. Insofar as this is true, I am an unquestionably accurate reporter. This is not the time and place for me to go into a deeper part of the wood, a profounder problem. I question myself too much. This is part of my personality. I seem to wonder *that* (not *if*) I exist. Of course, it was toward this basic question that all my work with Dr. Emerson was heading. But for a long time I did not know I felt any doubt of myself in the ultimate meaning of the two words, "doubt" and "myself."

He never made a mistake with me. Of course, a quibbler might question my conclusions. As Edith said, he couldn't lose, for if he did not sigh when I must have driven him up a wall with tedium, I concluded he was sparing me for a reason. When he did sigh, I concluded he was not sparing me for a reason.

I bring up the above intentionally.

I respect Dr. Emerson so very much. Almost everyone respects his doctor, even if it's just someone who cures an itch with an ointment. I suppose we all endow the people we need with more beneficence than they would ever claim for themselves.

But this respect was necessary too. It made it possible for me to bring myself to him.

I never got to this point with Dr. Evan Ness. Of course, I only saw him a few times, and I am running on ahead of the story. There is such a thing as rapport. I just never made this rapport with Dr. Ness, even though he was recommended by Emerson. With Emerson the rapport had been natural and immediate.

What still seems mysterious to me is this: Did I create him? Dr. Emerson? Did I create the help I needed?

You see what's wrong with my kind of mind? I was so *detached.*

While I was under treatment, getting myself straightened out, why was I studying his methods, his techniques, if indeed they were techniques? If I was so aware of his manipulation of me, what did it mean about me?

Did it mean only that I was percipient? Of course I'm perceptive; it's my business to be perceptive. That's what art is all about. But wasn't my perceptiveness defensive? Did I guard myself with perceptiveness? If so, is this why I was so aware of his actions? In other words, did my awareness of his methods prove I was resisting getting down to the crux of my problem? Did I observe him so carefully in order to avoid seeing myself?

Can anyone so aware of how he is being manipulated forget himself long enough to be caught unawares by a realization which can lead to a new self-awareness?

It was my own mind which stood in the way of my coming to know myself better.

It is a common problem. Now that I am wise to it, I see it all around me, in the way people cope with their lives.

I was always watchful, watching. All eyes. You learn a lot by watching. It's no wonder I'm in the visual arts. Yet my eyes were still filled with motes.

Love is blind, they say, and I was both blind with love and blind to what love meant to me. I had spent so many years of my life looking outward for signs of love, I was like a house that was all windows. I manned the windows, my eyes, my awareness. The room behind me was empty, for all my life was spent at the windows—a condition, a way of being, I took for granted, since I'd never known any other.

I did not know this then. I felt I had a little power over Dr. Emerson because I could read what he was doing to me. One-upmanship. I held on to this meager control probably because I am afraid of my feeling of powerlessness. I respected him and knew why I respected him, and though there were times I wondered if I had imagined his qualities of responsibility and professionalism, surely I believed in myself enough to believe I saw what I saw. I said this to myself.

I said this to myself. What an ordinary five words, strung together every day by people who say, I said to myself, I'm going to turn over a new leaf, or, I'm going to return that pair of shoes I bought. But think of what it means: I said to my own self. I said to me. The meaningfulness of this phrase lies beyond the wildest reaches of ordinary intercourse. I grasp that meaning, and my mind is stretched open to the skies. But our routines close in, and the skies turn into a ceiling. I said to myself this morning, This coffee is making me jittery. There, I used my revelatory phrase with the carelessness of any currency, a dull coin of language falling leaden between two cups of coffee and some toast.

Edith was clearing away the breakfast dishes. She said, "I haven't told you I really am enjoying my dressmaking lessons. I am very happy again." She kissed the top of my head. She has none of the angers, healthy or otherwise, of a Fem-Libber.

I knew what she was saying. She was saying, I'm sorry I made that scene the other night, I hate to be that kind of person, and I want you to know that everything is all right again, and that I am myself again. She is so unspoiled, I ache for her, my undemanding wife who loves me desperately.

I am myself again, she was trying to say. Please forgive me for not being myself the other night when I called you a cold fish.

But I realize Edith is never fully herself—which fills me with love and pity and sorrow. I know she could be something more. But since she doesn't know and since it doesn't hurt us—Edith or Amanda or me—that she doesn't know, since she is not struggling to know, I suspect Edith will be exactly as she is when she is a geriatrics case. When she was angry that night, she was probably more herself than she will ever realize. She was fighting for herself, for her own needs. There is nothing wrong with that.

From breakfast I went to Dr. Emerson's. It was a beautiful day in the beginning of spring. I hated to go indoors, to turn inward, to burrow when all the world was turning its face to the sun.

"I am on the brink of a big deal," I told him. "This is the biggest single thing that's ever happened to me."

For the past month I had been the focus of Cornelius Samuel Dexter's attention, the tuna and salmon mogul who has turned his Westchester estate into a growing museum. His adviser used to be assistant curator at the museum up in Boston which bought one of my early scenes. Mr. Dexter, through his adviser and even through his lawyer (I suppose magnates do everything through lawyers and personal agents), tentatively and then overtly and personally suggested that I execute a large work for him, something which he could feature on his estate. He didn't care how big it was, he told me in an exchange of telephone calls. He would have a building constructed to house it if necessary. He said he found my work compelling; that was his word. He said my re-creation of reality (unlike painted oversize beer cans, which he also collected and found interesting historically) *was* reality itself at the same time that it was art. My work, he said, was both compelling and neo-romantic. I didn't agree with the second adjective, but I was not so stupid as to argue.

"He's read Schlossberg, obviously," I told Dr. Emerson. My shakes were now mixed with jitters of euphoria. "Schlossberg's reviews on the art scene set a lot of people's teeth on edge, but I find them stimulating, even if I don't quite follow them. But I do know he has a fantastically subtle mind, a creative-critical mind, which is a unique combination. Sometimes he creates a whole new school of painting through his reviews. He seems to know what the artist is doing before the artist can really say what he himself is doing. He sees relationships and trends as they are being born. He creates the scene as he reports on it, so that he *can* report on it, which can be dangerous. But Herman Schlossberg is first rate. He likes my work."

I believe Dr. Emerson has a certain affection for me. He seems to enjoy my conceit. I suppose conceit in an unconceited person is delightful. And I'm mad for him myself.

"Dexter," I said, "has invited me up to his place. I'm to start thinking in terms of what I want to do, but he thought I should see the space he has before I get down to actual work. I think it's his devious way of trying to influence me. He probably has a room already allocated for anything I do. And he thinks if I see the room first I'll do something which will just fit into it. However, I'm not going to let anything keep me from doing exactly what I want to do.

"I'm going up this weekend with Edith and Amanda. I'm taking them, at his suggestion, for the day. He may not be home himself more than an hour, but McHugh, the curator, will be there.

"If this thing goes through, I really will be made. Magazine articles, newspaper coverage, other collectors. Nothing succeeds like success. Edith thinks I ought to think of giving up Party Packages, but I don't see why I should. I can handle both. I really am on top of everything, so why put all my eggs in one basket. I really enjoy killing myself with work."

"You feel more secure when you are killing yourself with work," Dr. Emerson said.

"I can't bear time on my hands, waiting around."

He waited around himself for me to continue.

"I waited around for that eighteen-year-old girl long enough. I said to myself, If she doesn't want to be pinned to me, as it were, at the end of two weeks, I'm just going to have to drop her. I just wasn't going to wait around any longer. She had another fellow on the string, and me. You know what she said to me a year later? 'You didn't give me a chance to find out, to find out who I wanted more.' "

I could see something was bothering Dr. Emerson.

"I had several other relationships in college and the two I've already mentioned before getting married. Some weren't really relation-ships, but you know, I'd be attracted to a girl at a party or strike up an acquaintanceship in a summer resort or a bookstore and date her a couple of times. I guess I always rushed things too much, and they got scared off. But I can't stand waiting around; the hoping part I find killing."

Dr. Emerson said, "You have been waiting around ten months now for Nan." I could see my apparent inconsistency had him stumped. Or at least he wanted me to think I had him stumped.

"But I've never been involved with a *married* woman before!" I argued, quite blind to what I was saying. "This is absolutely the first time I've ever been involved with a *married* woman."

"You mean to say that if you'd discovered soon after you fell for Nan that she was single, you wouldn't have hung on all this time?"

"Of course not. I really can't stand not being sure. A single girl might be doing anything while I wasn't with her. A married woman is just with her husband, so I know where I stand. Even so, it's practically unbearable."

My logic was irrefutable. Neurosis is not irrational at all. It has its own system of reason. It knows exactly what to do to perpetuate itself. A twisted handling of reality works hand in glove with the drive to survive.

A neurosis is an adaptation, a complicated, astute adaptation. It helps you to survive in a difficult world. But the you that survives—twisted, barnacled, musclebound, yet only partially realized—doesn't know quite how to live. Living is quite different from surviving, as different as existence is from truly being. This is my understanding of the whole trying business.

"The hopelessness then of your situation with Nan gives you a sense of security," he said.

"It's hope, it's hope," I repeated, for he had apparently not got the point which we'd touched on some time ago, "it's hope I can't stand."

"Hopelessness is better, though not much?"

"Of course."

"Since you don't believe you'll ever possess Nan, you can bear her obvious rejection of you. If you don't get her, you can square it with yourself by saying it's because she's married. If you didn't get a single girl, you'd have to face up to what you'd failed to get for yourself, what you would have lost."

"You're so wrong," I said. "Nan has not rejected me yet. She's coming around."

I had several things to bring him up to date on. "I had coffee with her again ten days ago, last Thursday and also yesterday. I told her I was going away. I didn't say I was spending the day in Westchester. I simply said, 'I'm going away,' and I watched her with every pore of my body.

" 'Oh, where?' she asked, casually enough, but those eyes of hers gave her away.

" 'Upstate. I don't know exactly when I'll be back,' which was true. I didn't know what hour on Sunday we'd leave Dexter's.

" 'I'll miss our coffee breaks,' she said.

"Overcome with gratitude and the pain of hope restirred, I didn't know what to say.

" 'One can get used to anything apparently,' she said mischievously. That was the first time I knew she had a sense of humor. I realized that the way she had conducted herself so far with me was her formal, wary, social self. I tell you she is beginning to loosen up. There's no question about it.

"A few days later I gave her a parting gift—a signed poster from an earlier period of my work. Mainly I gave it to her because I hoped she'd ask me to put it up. You know I've never been inside her office. From the glimpse I've had of it at the door, all I've seen are books and an ungainly avocado plant.

"She took it, looked at it carefully, thanked me and then rolled it up again. I had the feeling she was both pleased and yet uncertain about what to do with it, so I said, 'It's to go over your desk. I have the right tacks for it. I'll put it up for you myself.' She didn't take me up on my suggestion. Perhaps she is afraid of having something of mine her husband, if he ever comes to visit, might ask her about. In any case, at my landing later, she thanked me very warmly, wished me a good trip and we shook hands. She let her hand stay in mine for a long time. I could have leaned six inches to the right and my mouth would have brushed her temple. I would have kissed her. She looked as if she would not have minded or been surprised."

My chest was distended with the agony of longing. I do not exaggerate. Why should I? I seem ridiculous enough to myself without playing up my folly. But the man who thinks he's in love *is* in love. Is there any other criterion? My hand happened to touch her upper arm. My whole body suppressed a cry. If only I can have her, I will be healed. Healed, made whole, delivered back to myself. Nan, why do you leave me so alone!

"She is never around weekends. From about four on Fridays to ten in the morning on Monday she is away. I have no idea where. I've tried to look up her name in the directory, but I have no inkling of what her husband's first name is, and the people listed with her last name have unlikely addresses." I never forgot myself long enough, however overwrought I became in my sessions with Dr. Emerson, to betray her last name. She was a married woman and I was the strait-laced guardian of her respectability. "Actually, there were two possibilities, one of an Edwin such-and-such and another of a William such-and-such, jeweler, with addresses uptown. I called both and asked for Nan. They had never heard of her, so I concluded she has an unlisted number. I was planning to hang up the moment she came to the phone. But it would have felt good at least to know where she disappeared to every night and every weekend.

"Last week I had an idea. As soon as she left on Friday, I went to the superintendent who lives in the basement and complained of a steady drip on the ceiling of my lavatory. I said I suspected a leak upstairs. He considers me the handiest tenant in the building, for when I moved in I had the old windows of my office torn out and I myself put in new ones. Those summers spent as a construction worker when I was a teenager have always stood me in good stead.

He gave me the key to Nan's place, trusting me to turn off the faucet or whatever. I had a copy of her key made even before I went up to examine the 'leak.' "

"Breaking and entering," Dr. Emerson commented flatly.

"I was entering, but I had no intention of taking a thing. I had a compulsion to see with my own eyes where she spent her time. I intended to surprise her by putting up my poster over her desk. I intended to tell her her faucet had been leaking, which was why I'd come in in the first place.

"Well, she didn't have a desk. She had two tables—a card table on which file folders were neatly placed, and a long deal table on which she had her typewriter, pencils, clippings, magazines, et cetera. It was so monastic, I was both amazed and tickled to the marrow. It was the kind of room a monk would have. There was this narrow bed with a denim cover on it, one sling chair besides the straight-backed one she sat on to work, the grimy avocado plant, and a hotplate on the windowsill. You see, she can make coffee for herself up there. She doesn't have to have coffee downstairs. So she must have coffee downstairs because she wants to run into me. I was so happy, I decided really to surprise her. I decided then and there to give her place a new coat of paint from ceiling to floor. I painted her walls a flat white and her floor a barn red. The difference it made to her place was fantastic. I did it all between four-thirty Friday and midnight Sunday. Edith thought I was finishing up a package job. I was exhausted, for of course I had to do the whole thing myself. I even put in a peephole for her. Over the deal table she has a board on which she's tacked reminders and clippings of poems, bits and pieces from magazines and newspapers. So I put my poster over the bed, which made more sense anyway.

"She came to work yesterday and did not take a coffee break. I watched at the door as much as I could but didn't see her go. The super came and said, 'I got no complaint personally, you understand. You can go ahead and improve the property all you like, but give me back that key.' He wasn't terribly upset, expecting almost anything from an artist.

"If she'd only let me see her place. She might have just once said, Come have a look. It's only a pad, but I love it, or something to that effect. I wouldn't have had to go to such lengths." But no harm's been done, I assured Emerson. It was Tuesday morning, and right after that session I was going to go to the office and find out if she liked her new paint job.

I found her in my office waiting for me. Miss Price was giving her dirty looks from where she had retired to get a load of bookkeeping done. I keep Miss Price very busy; it's getting so I may have to get in another girl, part time anyway.

"Don't deny what you've done!" was the first thing Nan said, her eyes blazing.

"Not for anything," I said. I felt more in control than ever before with her and, as she was talking, I realized why. There was something of me up there in her place. I'd left something there of myself: my flat white paint, my barn red, my poster. My initiative, my hard work, my sweat. I had left something there to be redeemed.

"These shenanigans have got to stop!" she cried. "I have no time for nonsense."

"It looks great, doesn't it?"

"I think you're off your rocker!"

"I am!" I cried happily. I'm beside myself because of you.

"If you keep this up, I'm going to tell my husband and then you'll be sorry."

"Your husband doesn't know about me?" I found this very interesting.

"My husband has important work to do. I don't bother him with nonsense! I can take care of myself, thank you. Not only will I tell him, I'm going to call your wife if you don't stop."

"You're a family wrecker!"

"*I'm* a family wrecker? You *are* out of your mind!"

"I didn't ruin anything of yours," I said.

"All I want is peace and quiet and time, time to write!" She was getting quite overwrought. I swear she was practically stamping her beautiful little feet. "That's all I ask for in this crazy world. If I weren't practically there—if I weren't just about to make it—I'd move out of here so fast. But I haven't the time to move. I simply don't have the time to take the time to move. So you just leave me alone!"

She stalked out. Miss Price shook her head.

"She's right about one thing. It is a crazy world with crazy people in it." She looked at me.

"Poets are notably unstable," I said. "Take Bob Meacham." I know Miss Price found him too much, hanging around the way he did. A grown man with time on his hands is almost disqualified from manliness, or so we feel in our culture. Miss Price is an upholder of puritan tradition. She's an updated Pilgrim spinster. It's a comment on me that I have had her working for me since Party Packages was formed.

"The shenanigans she referred to are all in her head," I said. I am clever, no question about it. "The shenanigans she's referring to have to do with my putting a peephole, an improvement, in her office, which she told me she needed, given the kooks who troop in and out of this building. She's the craziest poet alive!"

Miss Price shrugged and threw up her hands. She's too unimaginative to indulge in speculation for more than ten seconds at a time.

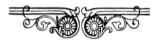

The following weekend Edith, Amanda and I went up to visit Cornelius Samuel Dexter. It was amazing, I told Dr. Emerson later. Reality never ceases to amaze me. Dexter was a little man of sixty, dapper, urbane, gimlet-eyed, cultivated. Yet he had worked his way up from a poor background (I've read in *Time* magazine his father was a dirt farmer who died during the Depression) with practically no formal education, until he became a king in the fish cannery business. He is obviously a driven man, and his drive to succeed in his field having been more than fulfilled, he is now driven to excel as a philanthropist with an interest in the arts. (He has endowed a hospital and an adoption agency.) His grounds were fabulous. I wished my artist friends could see them. Most of them have no idea at all how fantastic reality can be. You'd think they of all people would know, but their imaginations seldom run rife in this area.

Edith did not enjoy the day as much as I did. When we left she said, "Slave labor built that place. He's like an old-time robber baron brought up to date. I couldn't live in a place like that in a million years."

"I could," I said, surprising myself. "Why not?"

"Just think of all the people he exploited in order to make the money that place represents."

"Those people needed the jobs in the canneries or they wouldn't have worked for him."

"I don't know anything about economics. But it's all wrong that one man should own all that."

"His giving it all up would not make a difference to people starving in Bolivia. He's a philanthropist anyway."

"I don't care. All I know is it goes against my grain."

"It doesn't go against my grain at all that he may be paying me twenty-five thousand dollars for whatever I come up with. I'm selfish, I suppose."

"You're more realistic than I am," she said, listening to what she said as if to detect a flaw in it.

We were walking away from his château (that is the only word for it), down a long drive of trees in spring bloom, like the double rows of trees the French have before their towns or larger villages. Our car, looking like an art object itself in this setting, an object suggesting a recent secondhandedness, a new relic, was at the end of the driveway. Amanda had run on ahead and was already curled up in the back seat when we reached it. The sun was setting and the sky hung like a huge Olitski across an expanse of golf course, Mr. Dexter's private property. We drove at least a quarter of a mile before we left his estate and turned onto the highway.

"I am quite realistic," I told Dr. Emerson. "But am I selfish? Or is Edith too selfless? Or what is selfishness anyway?"

Dr. Emerson looked brightly out of his face. I could almost see the young boy he must have been, peering over a wall at someone else's apple trees. Peering and hoping to discover some unexpected activity next door. Wasn't this what he made a living at doing now? "What does selflessness or selfishness mean to you?"

"My mother said I was selfish when I was young. I knew it was bad to be selfish, but now I'm not sure."

"Yes?"

"She said it was selfish of me to want my father to stay at home when his patients needed him."

"Your father wasn't home much?"

"She said she'd had to make certain adjustments to his schedule and be more selfless about it all. She said to be selfless was very important. To forget about yourself and *yet* be very independent. She's always been full of a certain amount of crap."

I was shocked by what had come out of my mouth. I had never realized I'd thought she was full of hogwash. I reeled a little, laughed, tried to recover myself quickly so that Dr. Emerson would not have any advantage over me.

"You did not believe she knew what she was talking about?"

"She knew what she was talking about. I was a little slow in understanding. She was actually saying one must be self-reliant. I must be self-reliant, and she too had to be self-reliant. It was because of my father's schedule that we had to be self-reliant. She was right then and even later. He didn't leave her much money when he died, and she was a fairly young widow, forty-seven, but she did not break down under the strain. She's quite a dame, coming to the big city and making out with this antiques store she owns in the Village. She is quite sure of herself, quite undemanding, quite selfless."

"If she is so sure of herself, perhaps she's not selfless. Perhaps these words must be defined."

"She doesn't want much of me—she's not selfish in that way. She's actually said, 'Your dad was lucky I was so resourceful. Inner resources, I mean.'"

"What do these terms, selflessness and selfishness, mean to *you?*"

"I'm quite unambivalent about being selfish. More so than Edith. I want success, all that's coming to me. I work for it, I put myself out for it, but frankly I want some returns for it. I think this is positive, healthy. It's an expanding universe and a still possibly affluent society —why shouldn't I take my place with the rest of the world?

"I don't expect anything for nothing, mind you. I put myself out for Nan, for instance, killing myself for her that weekend, but I want something in return. I don't deny it. I'm realistic." But now it was I who was dealing out some hogwash. I had not put myself out for her because I wanted something in return. That would have been healthy. I put myself out because I felt I would expire if I didn't.

"I'm putting myself out right now, thinking about a *chef d'oeuvre* for Dexter, something that will knock him off his feet. Something that will hold its own on that place of his. It can't be puny. It can't be too subtle, too harmonious. It's got to be felt, be conspicuous. It's got to take its place among those large Moores, Rickeys and Nakians he's got, not to mention the Bontecous. He does go in for the lyricists."

"What does holding your own mean?" Hadn't he asked me this once before?

"It means being something, being someone, along with all the other someones."

He seemed pleased.

"I'm somebody now. But I'm going to be an even more important somebody, unless I gum up the whole works, my whole life, because of Nan. You know something, I already know what it is I'm going to be making for Dexter. It came to me as we were driving home in the early evening. I was so excited, I could hardly drive. I felt close to the truth, that truth I'm always looking for, trying to say through my work."

"You are definitely trying to say something through your work," he said again. It drove me up a wall then, this dullness of his which showed itself occasionally. Of course I was trying to say something through my work, who doesn't, I wanted to exclaim.

"We were passing a winding row of houses, lighted up by lamps and lights over their front doors. Second-floor lights were being turned on here and there, haphazardly yet almost rhythmically. These homes, which glowed with coziness and intimacy, unknown intimacies, I was glad we were fleeing from in our car. They were monuments to love and children and yet I was glad we, we passengers in our car, were fleeing the scene, so to speak. This is how my mind worked. The scene. I am the creator of appearances or scenes. Each of these homes was a scene, of course. So far I'd created porches, bedrooms, a corner of a nursery. Now I knew what I must make for Dexter's collection. I must assemble a whole house (he had promised to have a building expressly constructed for one of my scenes if it required that much space). But my new work would be a house itself. It would be a frame house with everything in it just like a house. It would not be a replica. It would be an object, a three-dimensional appearance. Every evening when the light faded outside, an electronic device would turn on the lights one by one. When Dexter and his guests looked out of his living-room window, they would see my house glowing across the rose garden. They would be able to walk up to it and look in on it the way evening strollers can catch glimpses of other people's lives through their windows. But if they really wanted to, they could also enter my scene, walk up the stairs and find themselves in a total environment. More and more people," I explained to Dr. Emerson, "are building objects that are environmental. The hugeness of our cities, cloverleaf intersections, buildings, bridges and other concepts made this inevitable." I was absolutely euphoric, thinking of my masterpiece.

"There are details to be worked out, of course, such as whether to have dummies in one or two of the rooms or to leave the rooms entirely empty. Lights going on gradually in a totally unpeopled house would have a compelling effect, an ominousness of its own. On the other hand, I might invent a dummy or two that in its very construction embodied memories—such as having them made of clear vinyl and having memories (actual miniature scenes) encased in the heart cavity. Not in the head, mind you, but in the body. Or I might paint shadows on the floor and on the wall behind a lamp, shadows but no people. Or I could fix up some kind of reel which would cast moving shadows coming down the stairs. Always coming down the stairs and never going up!"

I was sent, released, telling him about my new idea.

"Why always coming down the stairs to the porch and never going up?" he asked. How did he know I intended to use a porch again?

"It's just an idea, I haven't gone into it all thoroughly yet. I'm just telling you possible ideas for further development. Nothing is resolved until it's completed. I haven't gone back to Dexter himself yet. I want him to think I'm struggling over the problem. He'll appreciate it more if he has to wait a bit before he hears from me. How's that for coping well!"

"In some areas you know how to cope very well," Emerson said.

"Darn tootin'."

He said nothing for a while.

"I stole something from my mother's store for Nan yesterday."

"First breaking and entering," he said. "Now stealing from your mother."

"I pay my mother for everything I need from her place. I paid plenty for the brass bed she was holding for me. But this lamp, this rickety thing with the beaded tassel, she's had since she sold our Poughkeepsie house. I wasn't about to ask her to sell it to me. I couldn't ask her to give it to me. So I stole it. I just took it. She'll never miss it. It's been behind a pile of junk for years."

"This lamp was in your old home?"

"It's three hundred years old, if it's a day," I said, exaggerating happily. "I used my duplicate key and left it in Nan's office. She needs a light by that bed of hers."

"Why couldn't you have asked your mother to give you the lamp?"

"She might not have agreed to it."

"If it was just part of a pile of junk, as you say, why shouldn't she have given it to you?"

"I just didn't feel like asking, but you're making too much of it. If you could see this lamp, you'd know it isn't worth discussing."

Actually, that lamp was most worth discussing, that lamp I stole from my mother to sneak into the office of the girl I loved. I snuck it out of one woman's place to sneak it into another woman's place. In my sneakers I did my lover's work. I had worked alone, not asking permission of the one or of the other. Strange manifestation of a lovesick soul! Light of my heart, Nan. Lamp of my mother's. One lights a lamp to hold back the darkness, to discourage fears, to create rooms full of warmth and tenderness. Hobgoblins keep away! A child read to by lamplight dreams of all that future before him, vast world of possibility and hope, all pleasure in the safety of amber light. Children (I see it in Amanda) are so small in two vast spaces: the world and the time which is to come. World, worlds; and time, limitless time. I gave Nan a gift of my whole self, in that moth-eaten rickety lamp, three feet high on insecure feet and about a foot in diameter.

I told Dr. Emerson, my voice almost breaking, "Nan came down the next morning with the thing in her hand. But her face was ecstatic, so I didn't know what to expect." Dr. Emerson himself did not see what was coming, I later found out.

" 'You're impossible!' she declared, plunking the lamp down by the door. She almost broke it. 'Where's that duplicate key?' She put out her hand. 'If you don't give me that key I'll call my husband this minute and the police as well.'

"I handed her the key. It was in my pocket. I didn't have to go look for it.

"Then she burst into a big smile. Her whole face arranged itself into the most ecstatic smile I've ever seen on anyone's face in my whole life. I thought, Women are unpredictable, but there isn't anything I can do about it.

"She said, 'I've got an option from Doubleday for my novel. My agent just called me up last night. My novel is being optioned by Doubleday!'

" 'What novel?' I asked." I could swear Dr. Emerson uttered the same words to me at the same time.

"What novel!" he asked in a loud voice.

" 'My novel,' she repeated to me. 'My very first novel. Doubleday is giving me an option contract. Five hundred down if they like the next hundred pages, say, and then we're off and running. The option becomes a contract if they like the first half. So far I've only three chapters I'm going to keep. I've thrown out a complete first draft. But that's par for the course.' "

I felt something was wrong with Dr. Emerson, as if he suddenly had stomach cramps or was making a supreme effort to stifle a sneezing spell.

" 'I'm not a poet, after all,' she said, brimming over with the joy of it all, and directing part of this toward the window where Miss Price was looking up from her work. 'You see, I'm still terribly nervous about it all. I do write and rewrite bits and pieces of poems. I *am* interested in poetry and I've had several published over the years. I still keep sending out poems I've written the last three years sort of as a good luck charm. Better the poems get rejected than my novel. You see, with a big project like a novel, it just feels better to say you do anything else at all rather than admit you are working on something that may take two years to complete. After two years it could fall flat on its face. I'm a real novelist now though. I have it in writing from Doubleday.' "

Dr. Emerson broke in. He must have been feeling croupy, his voice was so strangled. "She's a novelist, you now say. Not a poet! Double-day!"

"It surprised me too. But that's what she told me just yesterday. She had told me she was a poet. She'd told Miss Price this at the beginning, you remember. But it turns out the little wench has been batting out a novel up there."

"Where is your office?" he asked. His eyes looked blank, stunned at some view I was unaware of.

"Between Second and Third on Fifty-fourth. Two sixty-nine East Fifty-fourth, to be exact. But I still want you to bill me at home. I don't want Miss Price to know I'm seeing a headshrinker. She'd think I was some kind of maniac.

" 'I suppose you don't have three children either,' I said to Nan.

" 'What children?' she asked, so happy she was *non compos mentis.*

" '*Your* three children.'

" 'Of course I'm the mother of three children,' she said. 'Now you just leave me alone.' And she left my office."

"Do you believe she has children?" Dr. Emerson asked, watching me as if his own life depended on it.

I didn't know what to say. She had claimed to be a poet, but she turned out to be a novelist. She had said she had three children, but maybe she didn't . . .

"Maybe she doesn't," I said lamely.

"Why, in your opinion, would she claim—" he asked.

"To impress upon me that she wasn't available, of course!" My own answer was all I needed to convince me she really didn't have three children, or any children.

"So she says her name is Nan, she's writing a novel for Doubleday, and she has no children."

These facts fascinated him as much as they did me. Did he think I was onto my real problem now? I had believed in lies. Was *that* my problem? Was simple gullibility my problem? Did I create something out of nothing to believe in? But she had told me she was a poet. Miss Price also thought she was a poet. Is one supposed to challenge what people tell you about themselves?

I don't remember going into much more with him that session. At his door he said, "Two sixty-nine East Fifty-fourth Street?"

"Please don't bill me anywhere except at home," I pleaded. "Miss Price would quit if she thought I was a nut, and I need her to do my bookkeeping."

I left realizing suddenly it was not the end of the month anyway, so billing was not in question. But I did not feel relieved; I felt peculiar, as if I'd left something undone, like leaving the water running to overflow a bathtub. Something was amiss. I felt someone knew I had a piece of spinach between my teeth which I myself could not see.

The next morning at eight the telephone rang. Edith was taking a shower; I answered it. It was Dr. Emerson, of all people. He said he was calling because he was going away; he was very sorry to be doing this so abruptly, but his health had been bothering him recently and his doctor said he must have a complete rest at once. He gave me the name of a psychiatrist he thought highly of. He had already briefed Dr. Evan Ness, and he implied that he thought I should take up with Dr. Ness without a break in my treatment.

I started to say several things, but nothing came out.

"I am very sorry, truly," he said. "But my health . . . You will find Dr. Ness just as helpful as I, perhaps even more so in your case."

"But when you come back—"

"Under the circumstances . . ." he started to say and then again, "I am quite ill. I'm truly sorry. Good-by."

I ran into the bathroom. Edith was pink and slippery-looking behind the white shower curtain. "Dr. Emerson is sick," I told her. "I feel awful." I had to raise my voice against the sound of the water. "He's sick and has to go away. I'm supposed to call up this Dr. Ness. I can't believe he's sick—so suddenly. How dreadful! I hope it's not a heart attack. He did look bad the last time I saw him. Dr. Emerson is sick." Poor Dr. Emerson, I thought. Poor man. And poor me. Poor me, most of all.

I really went into a tailspin. I may have transferred, as they say. I felt abandoned and deprived. After almost nine months with him, he had thrown me out like a foundling. For a day or two all I felt was loss.

Nine months and I wasn't certain I'd learned anything at all from Emerson. I'd resisted rather successfully, one could say. I'd talked volumes, tomes about my work, about creativity (which one can go on about interminably), about my pitifully unrequited courting of Nan. Step by step, I'd gone over every exchange, every glimpse I'd had of her, twice, three times. We'd touched on certain other subjects, which were to become themes. But I didn't realize that any themes at all had been handled like the warp and woof on a loom. The design had not yet appeared. All I'd got was a taste of some carping back and forth.

Then I got angry with Dr. Emerson. (Like Edith, I too have been slow to get angry.) Bitterly angry that he'd thrown me out like a foundling. I felt at the same time terribly guilty to be angry—the usual complex of feelings. Actually, I was doing myself a lot of good getting angry. Only I didn't know it. Even his abrupt departure, his abrupt abandonment of me, was acting inadvertently as part of the treatment he'd terminated. Was he a genius? Or is there something truly occult about analysis? Or was I immaturely expecting miracles and finding one where it did not exist?

Small wonder I thought, as I have already stated, that I could not get away from his presence. What he had started in those fifty-minute hours I was continuing, or rather, since it seemed to have a life of its own, it was still going on inside of me willy-nilly.

Three weeks went by. I told Edith I was through with analysis. I was cured, I said. My anger sort of settled me. It passed quickly through my mind once: Maybe this was the way all psychiatrists ended their treatments. They simply threw the patient back into the sea, like a gasping fish, and said, You came up for air. All right. But get back into life now. Swim, on your own. You were so furious, you found you swam very well. However, I didn't really believe this could be true. I also began to suspect that Nan was not married. She must be single. She was single, a novelist, and had no children.

I spent part of that three weeks shadowing her. During the period that I entertained the thought she was single, true to my own dissection of my behavior, I kept myself on the qui vive. A certain added fear, matched only in strength by my anger against Emerson, hovered in my chest. I was like someone testing the security of a rundown wooden bridge. I wanted to cross on it, but I wanted to be ready (in case she *did* turn out to be single) to pull myself back in time. I was afraid to go too far out but compelled to find out how far was too far. I teetered, driven but ready to brake myself, over the abyss.

She barricaded herself behind her door. No coffee breaks, nothing to interfere with her work. I could see she was thinking of nothing but her novel. She went up and down the stairs like a sleepwalker. She most decidedly had the correct number of rings on her left hand: a good-sized solitaire and a gold wedding band. Well, anyone can buy a wedding band, I told myself. The diamond could be an heirloom. I didn't know what I really wanted to believe.

That was the rock-bottom worst of it. *I did not know what I wanted to believe.* Whatever I believed would undo me further.

I suspended belief. While I was at it, I also suspended disbelief.

For a while I actually stopped shaking. Incidentally, my shaking had let up a bit since the time I first started with Emerson, but now it stopped completely for two whole weeks. Edith noticed it first. She served wine at dinner to celebrate. Just the two of us finished off two bottles of Châteauneuf-du-Pape.

A while later Bob Meacham was around again and having a bite with us. He reappeared, as he usually did a couple of times a summer, on his way to, from or around his bachelor hunting grounds. As I have said, Bob has his way with the girls. As I was opening our apartment door, I could tell he was swinging Puttykins through the air by her delighted but bloodcurdling screeches. Edith had put on her newest Swedish cotton, or is it Finnish? Anyway, when I entered the apartment, she, dressed in a viridian green smock, was downing a martini, and a two-headed human was approaching me. It gave me quite a turn. The two-headed creature sorted itself out into Bob Meacham and my daughter. She was on his back, kicking his ribs.

"Dad-dee!" my offspring said.

"You look great. Splendid, sir," Bob said, dipping suddenly so Puttykins screeched again. I knew at once Edith had told him I was cured and through with Emerson. Who knows what else they said about my problems or what they thought my problems were. He hadn't even looked at me with his listening eyes, so how did he know I was great, splendid. He liked that word "splendid"; pronouncing it made his sensual mouth curl as if he was swallowing paste.

I suppose I looked none too pleased. A husband may know intellectually that his best friend arrived only seven minutes ahead of him, but it feels emotionally as if the wife and the friend have been having some kind of intimate ball all afternoon.

Edith, sensitive as always, sensed my resentment. "I've made your absolutely favorite dinner!" she announced cheerily. "It took me all afternoon, but it turned out splendidly," she said, telling me I was wrong to think what I was thinking. But I was no longer thinking it. Edith is not Bob's type, and she's basically afraid of him. He's too sure of himself. She knows I know this. I know she knows I know this. God, we do live mirrored in each other's perceptions! Nevertheless, she can't help reacting guiltily, masking that guilt in a remark which tactfully, cheerfully is a love offering.

"Splendid," I said, and having used the word, felt part of the gang at once. "You've been drinking too much beer again," I said to Bob, slapping his paunch.

He swung Puttykins down and flung himself to the floor to do some push-ups. We don't go in for any intellectual conversation and don't miss it either. I must admit that discovering the basic ingenuousness of the so-called creative person helped me grow up fast when I was about twenty-five. I'd been accepted for the first time by this artists' colony in Vermont (where Bob and I first met almost twelve years ago) and had anxiously hoped I'd measure up to the rest of the inmates, the other artists. I spent a month or so before going up, boning up on the names of art movements and philosophies, artists of the Italian Renaissance, who-was-who among American contemporary giants, et cetera. But it didn't take more than a couple of meals in the commons, as we called it, to discover that the conversation of artists, writers and composers is chiefly gossip about other artists, writers and composers.

Sometimes the juiciest tidbits were about critics or conductors or absent (from that particular colony at that particular time) artists. But just because someone was present did not preclude our talking about him. What was required (since we were gallant) was that he or she, as the case might be, be seated at another table. By the third meal I knew who had been in Casablanca living with whom (both male) and was now here and drinking in whose (male, of course) studio at three in the afternoon when he should have been working. It was less clear why a certain fiftyish and too-plump sculptor, a woman, had been able to monopolize a certain handsome man of thirty, until it had been carefully explained to me (they all found me naïve up there that first summer) that he, the thirty-year-old music critic working on his first book of essays, was almost completely blind. He could not feel paintings with his hands, someone said, but he could appreciate sculpture, and what he liked to do was to feel this plump lady's work. That is what they claimed at the colony that summer.

I'll never know, but my beard and calabash pipe must have come in for their share of interpretation. When I became more mature, I gave up both protective affectations.

Creative people are like agents in an underground movement. Spies, agents, guerrillas don't have to assert, every time they meet, the nature of their commitment. If they didn't believe in the cause, they would not be gathered together in an enclave. The esprit de corps of all art colonies is high because of a basic assumption: Needless to say, we are all artists, whether young, old, first rate or mediocre; needless to say, each is working on his project. For once we can forget we are artists. No one at these colonies finds anyone else unique, a sacred cow or a provocative freak. We work all day, and then we meet for supper and behave as we want to behave—like people. This means we get in all the gossip we can and tear down as many reputations as we know how to. Though, of course, we are united when other people, the laity, ridicule one of us. Which makes sense; it takes a relative properly to slander another relative. I love Bob Meacham, and when I have said he was infantile, I was not criticizing his poetry, which is of a high caliber, nor questioning his artistic integrity, which is unimpeachable, nor his personal probity, to which I can swear. I have simply been saying he was immature where women are concerned. As Dr. Emerson would put it, he was immature not in regard to his work but in regard to love, to relationships. (But now I am not certain at all what I think of Bob.)

"What young girl's moral fiber have you been threatening since we three last forgathered?" I asked, sounding pedantic to myself when I had hoped to be sardonic. Bob has a reputation for seducing an all-too-willing student a term up in Rochester where he teaches, though he flatly denies any such crimes against nature.

"It ain't their moral fiber I'm after," he said. My wife laughed.

"Do they come topless to class?" I asked.

"If you've seen two, you've seen them all," he said.

"That is *not* original!" Edith exclaimed triumphantly. Women do enjoy male conversation more than males do female talk. And they love to hear men talk about other women.

"The girls I teach are nubile and strictly middle class," he said. "They think I'm old. I—I in whom the undying flame still blazes. Anyone over twenty-five is a granddaddy. What is this country coming to!"

"I read that in *Time,*" said Edith, who subscribes to some conservative magazines as well as a bevy of liberal ones. Dissenters have to know what they are dissenting from. " 'If you've seen two, you've seen them all.' That's pretty sharp for *Time.*"

"If you've seen two," he repeated, "you long for some sophistication. Most of the girls upstate are creatures, gorgeous, nubile creatures, without any idea of what it means to be human. They are not human. Not that they are subhuman, like apes. There's nothing wrong with an intelligent, feeling ape. It's not that. They aren't bobcats or sheep or leggy gazelles. They are simply nothing at all, filled like balloons with gaseous secondhand ideas about art, astrology, literature, sex, satanism, detergents, a second car in every garage, and the swinging life. Mind you, I haven't come across a single firsthand reaction to Drano even. Only secondhand hand-me-down ideas from television or the movies or some rubbishy reading list their freshman adviser waves in front of them. I long for some sophistication, for something real. You know, it's sophisticated to be real. It's really very worldly to be real." No, I'd never known that, but I recognized that he was right.

Nan is very real. So real she hadn't been afraid to repulse me. She has had no need to prove she is desirable, and so she had not even given me the time of day. ("My time is very important to me.") She is very sophisticated, very real. She hadn't been at all impressed with having an admirer, at least not yet; she was too worldly to care for such kid stuff. She was more interested in producing a firsthand idea of life as she saw it, a novel. Bob's thesis applied to her perfectly.

"Maybe you're ready to settle down again," said my wife, who believes in marriage. Bob had been divorced at least five years and, to Edith, had been a potential husband for several of her girl friends, all of whom Bob had conspicuously ignored.

"Did I tell you I'm being named for the Pulitzer?" Bob said by way of answer. His work always had come before everything else, which is part of his charisma where women are concerned. Frank Sinatra's power lies in the fact that he seems to belong to himself. He is not watching a woman to see how he stands with her. As a result, it is she who is forced to do the watching.

"Congratulations!" I exclaimed. I always knew he'd make it.

"I'm just one of several named. But it doesn't hurt and it might turn out to be just splendid."

"The trouble with you," I said, with my new education at my fingertips, "is not where your work is concerned. What does love mean to you?"

He growled. Edith ate it up.

"Besides sex?" I pursued.

He growled some more.

Amanda, who'd been hiding in the closet waiting for Bob to catch on to her game, came back into the living room and climbed onto uncle's lap. "Do it again," she ordered. He growled again. She didn't look out of place on another man's lap, I noted with a dismay I suppressed; neither did he look out of place with a young child on his knee. His son Jim must be at least ten years old now.

"You ought to get married and have some more kids," I said flatly. "This infantile stuff you go in for is ridiculous."

He spread his hands apart. "I have no designs on your little one. After what I've just said, how can you think I'm after Lolitas?"

"What does love mean to you?" I asked him, in a fair imitation of Dr. Emerson's manner.

"Love is life, brother!" he exclaimed, squeezing the life out of my daughter. "Life. Life. Life." Puttykins kept squealing.

Well, he'd given himself away all right.

The difference between me and Bob Meacham is simple. He's healthy.

Bob's thirty-nine, divorced, father of a ten-year-old he rarely sees, and not about to get married soon again, but he's healthy. I'm married and a father, and by all conventional standards I should be normal, whatever that means. But, unless he's still stalking women at fifty and making a fool of himself when his belly is even bigger with beer, he has never been lovesick. He has relationships with women which might be called lovewell but not lovesick. There was a chance, I thought that day, he'd reveal his condition later on. There was nothing to do but to wait and see, like waiting for a culture under a microscope to sprout erratic cells.

It was this visit from Bob Meacham which sent me back into analysis. Not right away. But he's been a recurrent incentive driving me further and further into an understanding of myself. Just a superficial incentive, of course, but certainly recurrent, as I was to discover again even later.

Bob visited us in June, I think. Around the end of July I got the shakes again. I slept all right, but as I think I'd once said to Emerson, though we never did go into it, I woke up different. Before the beginning of my troubles, I had always been a deep sleeper and a reluctant riser. I got to work, because I'm disciplined and responsible, by nine-thirty every day, but it was always an effort. When I began my shaking and lost my appetite, I also found I'd become a light sleeper. I slept "on top of the bed," so to speak. I never really lost my bearings in a really deep sleep. Consequently, every morning at seven I simply opened my eyes to find I was fully awake. Had I been up half an hour and had had a cold shower and several cups of coffee, I could not have been more wide awake. I concluded that I really hadn't slept in a year. Certainly I hadn't slept in the way I'd slept all my life before that. And I'd never had a dream to bring to Dr. Emerson the way students bring their teachers apples. That fact alone shows the state I was in.

First I called Dr. Emerson. I couldn't help it. I had to dial his number. But his phone had been temporarily disconnected. So he was really ill and had left town. I felt, in my characteristic way, both better knowing this and worse. I decided to call Dr. Ness. He answered. It might have been August second or third. After I introduced myself and mentioned Dr. Emerson, he said, "He briefed me on you two, three months ago, but I'm going on vacation tomorrow for six weeks. If you like, I can recommend another doctor for the interim—"

I interrupted him. I didn't want to go so far afield, I said. (Dr. Ness was a link to Dr. Emerson; still another doctor would take me into outer space, or so I felt.)

He interrupted me in turn. "It slipped my mind, everyone's on vacation until Labor Day. The best I can do for you is to make an appointment with me for September eighteenth at four o'clock."

I felt like the dying light in the middle of a television set right after the picture has been turned off. The light traveled and shrank as though the spectator were being left years behind. Was I the fading light or the abandoned spectator?

"Dr. Emerson did tell me about you," he said pointedly, as if to give me something to hang on to.

"I need him," I said.

"Mr. Safford, I will be here waiting for you September eighteenth at four. All of us go on vacation in August. I'm sorry, but this happens to be a fact."

Facts. I am a grownup man of thirty-seven now, successful, married, responsible, honorable, imaginative, creative, sought after by a tuna and salmon mogul, loved desperately by my wife, needed by my daughter, the sole source of Miss Price's total income. I felt like nothing. I felt like a big zero. I felt this nothing was dying.

How do you account for emotions?

I had to get to the bottom of it. I said to myself, Even if I feel slightly better again, as I had for that two weeks in June, I must remember how I feel today, and keep doing something about it, until I am all better. My mind said this to my being. It was a promise I was to keep.

Nan was away on her vacation. The girl I'd never had, in any sense of the word, was away, and I was ready to die. She slipped away from me and didn't come back until September tenth. I had no idea when she was coming back, since she didn't bother to keep me posted. For five and a half weeks I simply was not myself. Edith said several times, "Emerson just didn't get down to brass tacks. See this Dr. Ness, if you must, but I still think you better look up Dr. Wright." She was very worried about me. For a couple of days I was back on the banana diet. I couldn't chew and swallow much else.

Meanwhile, back at the ranch, as they say, life went on. Edith was pregnant again. This time she'd only had to use the thermometer three, or was it four months?

On the strength of her pregnancy, I made a resolution. When Nan came back (the super told me she had paid her rent through September), I was simply *not* going to pursue her any more. I could not square it with myself that an adult human being, on the way to becoming a father again, should carry on in sneakers and hang around doors. I wasn't going to have it. I was going to get myself straightened out.

I didn't want to have to start again with a total stranger, this Dr. Ness, and have to recapitulate everything Emerson now knew. On a hunch, I called up Emerson a couple of days before the eighteenth. He picked up the phone.

"Dr. Emerson!"

"Yes?"

"George Safford."

"I understand," he said quickly, "you are seeing Dr. Ness the day after tomorrow."

"I want to see you."

"I have a backlog of work—after my illness—and can't fit you in."

"But you are my doctor. You know all about me. How do you feel, by the way? Are you all right?"

"Fine, thank you. I'm sorry but my schedule is absolutely full."

"I did a lot of thinking while you were sick. I have thought my way through. I've given up on Nan. I simply can't throw my life away on her."

He was silent for a moment longer than normal. Was this silence a working silence, or simply a social one? He couldn't take me on as a patient, so it was probably just a natural, human pause.

"Nevertheless," he said. "Nevertheless, Dr. Ness is expecting you.

I am sorry," he reiterated with emphasis, "but I am not able to fit you in."

"You were so right about the whole Nan business. I was practically cracking up over a nothing affair. She's back on the scene now, and do you know I haven't gone to the door once to listen or to watch. I think I've made a big breakthrough."

"I am very happy," he said warmly. "I am happy everything is turning out to your satisfaction."

Something about Dr. Emerson will not let me go. I may have assigned him a maturity and power that is all in my head, but I doubt it. He is a totally relaxed, very secure, practically all-seeing person who knows exactly what he is about. Well, almost exactly. His security gives him a great economy of speech and attitude. Except for the fact that he is a thin, tall, almost handsome man, with nearsighted eyes which give him a certain amount of trouble, I would say he had an overweight, placid Buddha-like quality. You can read a thousand variations into a Buddha's one enigmatic, confident, self-knowing expression. Dr. Emerson knew where I was going, so he simply made no mistakes—where I was concerned. He has always behaved perfectly about and toward me.

I went to Dr. Ness for two weeks. Nothing happened. I spent most of those two weeks telling him about my new commission for the estate of Cornelius Samuel Dexter. I had to weave back and forth chronologically to bring him up to date on my work, career and personal résumé. It was an unmitigated bore. I talked so fast, trying not to waste time on material which I'd already covered, I was virtually incoherent. Several times he had to stop me, and I had to repeat what I thought I'd said clearly the first time. This slowed me up even further, which frustrated me beyond endurance. I was pent up enough sticking to my resolution not to pay Nan, sitting over my head, any attention without having to cope with an analyst who seemed to be slow-witted. Dr. Ness was more paternal-looking than Emerson, but he seemed empty to me—bland and empty. Maybe he seemed empty because I brought him nothing of myself. With Emerson I felt I was getting through, communicating. Since this is the whole point of analysis, I decided to call Dr. Emerson again. I explained it all to him.

"Perhaps Dr. Ness is not for you," he said. "But there are other doctors."

"Can't you please find time for me! My life is going great guns. I'm through with Nan. The plans for the 'house' I'm building for Dexter are almost completed. I'm swinging into Christmas orders at Party Packages, and I'm going to be taking on more help. In a year or two I suspect I'll be farming out the work to a small factory. What I want is to get down to brass tacks"—Edith's expression—"and simply get rid of the possibility of ever repeating myself with another Nan."

"That is very sensible." I could tell he was thinking something through, perhaps taking into account the possibility of another patient's completing his treatments, so he would have time to fit me in.

"Edith is pregnant again, and I'm going to be a father for a second time."

"Is there another Nan?"

"Oh no. There's only one Nan, of course. But my problem is obviously with what she represents rather than with who she actually is."

"Well," he said. "You have been doing a lot of thinking, haven't you?"

"You really think so!"

Silence.

"I couldn't be more through with Nan. Now it's a question of making sure I don't go looking for another unapproachable girl."

After I said that, I don't remember how he put it, but he suggested (he had two hours available after a bit of juggling) that I resume my treatments with him. I have leavings of Sunday-school religion in me. I thought, This is my reward for really controlling myself with the dame upstairs. It felt so good to be taken back under Dr. Emerson's wing, I felt as if I'd been adopted out of an orphanage by a perfect father.

"People are so creative," I told him when I saw him again. "People's idea of creativeness is so limited, it surprises me. Edith is creating a life, yet she isn't at all anxious about the whole process. She's more anxious to prove that she won't need a baby nurse when the kid's born. She's more anxious to prove she can handle the baby and a three-year-old single-handedly a week after the birth. We can afford help, and I'm going to insist on it, but it'll be a fight all the way. I don't even know if I'm right. Maybe she'll do something awful simply out of guilt and tension; maybe I should let her kill herself with both kids. Who knows? I never am sure of anything."

"Sometimes you're quite sophisticated," he said.

"Do you really think so?" I felt half healed just being back with him. "I know my wife all right. She demands so much of herself, it hurts."

"You share some of the same weaknesses," he said.

I thought his remark over for a moment, but nothing occurred to me. I *did* demand a lot of myself? No, nothing came to me, so I continued: "Creativity is not limited to artists or to people who invent new equations or systems. We create our lives, our selves with every decision we make or inclination we express. Everyone is creative." I didn't know I felt this until I'd said it. The words for thoughts I'd only half thought came pouring out. I really could communicate with Emerson.

"Your taking me back feels to me strangely creative. You're helping to create a healthier me to lead a healthier life. You are, in a sense, writing my story!" What prophetic words. They make my hackles rise. Neither of us saw that both of us were getting deeper into a mixed-up case that could be unique in the annals of psychiatry.

"When we get married to someone, we are creating a particular marriage, not any other possible marriage. Or take the little man with a neighborhood repair store—he has created something, a necessary service, where nothing used to be. He may be living at the peak of his creativity, but for his son he may be creating unendurable limitations. Parents create the atmosphere in which their children's psyches are being invented."

"Would you say you were brought up in a relaxed household?" Dr. Emerson asked, apparently having decided to land *in medias res* with both feet.

"My parents loved each other very much. They were terrifically romantic about their marriage, much more so than Edith and I are. It had the quality of Abélard and Héloïse, or Peter Ibbetson, or Tristan and Isolde."

"A quality of myth?"

"They believed in it, so it wasn't myth."

"Did you believe in it, in the romantic quality of their love?"

"I am never sure what to believe in." Then I said before he could, "You know that is part of my problem. They may have been simply creative too, creating an overpowering love, for better or worse, till my father's death did them part. If they thought they were madly in love, they were madly in love. That I know is true."

"But did *you* think they were madly in love?"

"There was no need to destroy what they had, to be destructive. Painters want to give the impression they may not know what they are doing, that they are innocent mediums of power and originality, used by art, just as romantic lovers feel love uses them and is stronger than them. My parents needed to suffer," I said.

"You thought it was destructive to hold an opinion about them they did not share?"

"Of course not. I stand up for myself in arguments all the time. Dexter has been dickering with me. Sam isn't a tycoon by accident. None of us is what we are by accident, though our births, within a given situation, are accidents. Our motivations are accidentally created by accidents, but what they are, given the premises, are inevitable. Sam—that's what I now call Cornelius Samuel Dexter—has this terrific drive not to be put down. He is still proving to himself that he's not a small man in any sense of the word. He is still proving to himself he's not five feet four, a dirt farmer's son, a high school dropout. He keeps trying to cut me back, but I'm holding my own. I know, I know," I said, "I'm standing up for myself, for my vision.

After all, it's me who's the artist. I don't need the dough, and though the job would put me on the map, I am not settling for anything except the absolute truth about what I want to say.

"I've sold him on the idea in general. My 'house,' my assemblage, is to be situated behind his château. The forty-foot-long window of his living room overlooks a dropped garden lined by rose bushes and enclosed by low stone walls. Beyond the garden there is a half-acre section of lawn. My scene is to be built there. He is underwriting all expenses, and they are considerable, and I'm naming my price: fifty thousand. What we're arguing about now is not its cost to him—he is above financial niggling. He thinks big. What we're arguing about now is the size of the front door."

"What is it that doors, that a door means to you?" Dr. Emerson asked.

"I'm not going to the door any more," I told him. "I'm through with Nan. The house is to be empty. No dummies, no figures like George Segal's, not even shadows of figures painted on the walls or floors, as I once contemplated. Just a single ever-running shadow descending the stairs to the front door.

"You see," I said excitedly, "the house lights are to be electronically controlled. The first light to go on in the house in the late afternoon or early evening is going to be the nursery light, then the bathroom light, then the kitchen light; after that, in order, the dining-room, the living-room and finally the porch light. When the living-room light goes on, the upstairs lights automatically go off. The running figure, the shadow, runs down the stairs in the dim light of the hallway. At ten in the evening the porch light automatically goes off. That, until the next evening, is the end of the appearance, my scene. The house will sleep in the darkness, as all houses do, a cavern of mystery tucked in on itself like a bird with its head under a wing."

I leaned forward in my chair. I looked into Emerson's face. "You see, I'm insisting that the front door be oversize. It's got to be out of proportion to the rest of the house. It's got to be big, looming, frightening. It is the one feature which will make this house non-representational. The meaning of this house is in that door, that oversize ominous door. I am insisting on it. Sam's problem is that he's small physically. The size of that door seems to him, I think, a comment on him."

"But it's not a comment on him?"

"It's a comment on me!" I cried. Why didn't he see, I thought.

"But you are tall."

"And quite helpless," I said.

Where did those three words come from? I, helpless, who stands up for himself at every opportunity? I asked Dr. Emerson about this.

He answered by saying, "This house of your childhood . . ." and waited. Then he said, "This house *is* your childhood."

I was on the verge and I took fright. I felt cold, as if standing in front of the open door of a butcher's frozen locker. Buried in me, buried in my ancient self, in my experience which is my self, was something that he, he, Emerson, wanted to rob me of, or so it seemed. Clues would turn up at regular intervals, but I was not a detective. Detectives have it easy; they know they are looking for a body or for stolen goods or for the criminal. Clues kept turning up, but I didn't know what I was looking for. However, Dr. Emerson was pointing out clues. I was supposed to add them up and say, Ah, there's been a theft here, and the thing burglarized is me, of all things! As I've already said, it boggles the mind, this whole business of straightening oneself out.

Emerson had pulled up the lid of a deepfreeze, wanting me to experience the quality of the cold so I could see how frightened I was. I cannot say I knew all this was going on. I can only say I reacted in a kind of helpless terror.

"I need my dreams," I said. "If you take my dreams from me, I'll die. I'll be wiped out. I won't be an artist any more. I'll die in every sense of the word, die." I wanted to cry out, to warn him against my violence. I would defend myself with violence.

"You are so right," he said calmly. "You have waking dreams."

"I haven't dreamed in months," I shouted.

"You don't remember," he said, "but I asked you some time ago to tell me any dreams you had, whenever you had them. You did not dream, you said. I say your work is a waking dream."

"I'm going to win the fight with Sam Dexter. He's got to understand why the door has to be too big."

Emerson has explained to me since that he was not attempting to rob me, only to release me. It was I who felt I would be bereft of my talent, my drive, my very self, if I saw and dispelled my ancient experience.

I heard what he'd just said a moment later and asked him incredulously, "You asked me to tell you dreams?"

"On several occasions."

Why should he have made this up? It proves what I've kept saying: I am reporting what transpired to the best of my knowledge, but my knowledge was affected by my problem.

Two or three sessions later I said, "I can't wait to go ahead and start collecting the things that are to go into the house. We won't start building until next spring. I'm not stealing anything from my mother's store," I said with a laugh. "But I am buying several pieces of furniture from her. She specializes in a lot of junk like the kind I associate with summer houses in the thirties. Rattan chairs, a modernistic—you know all that word conjures—sideboard and end tables. Things with tacky geometric designs, the works. I wish I could get started right away while this idea is bugging me. But Sam still—"

"Why don't you explain to him what the door, the size of the door means? If he understood, he might agree."

"That's a great idea," I told Emerson, but I didn't know what I meant.

I came back the next week and said to Emerson, "You must be a fortuneteller or something. He did agree. I'm to get right with it. He saw at once when I told him why."

"What did you tell him?"

I looked at Emerson, this man who mirrored me, who reflected me back to myself, but better than an ordinary silvered section of glass can do. He mirrored me and at the same time helped me read what the reflection said. My work was a reflection of me too. I really was seeing double as I acted out my life.

I said slowly, very slowly, painstakingly, "I told Sam that the door had to be too large because it felt enormous to the shadow who kept running down the stairs. The door is enormous, see; the shadow is small. In the hall light the shadow is weak, very weak. The spectator almost thinks he is imagining the running shadow. The spectator realizes the presence of the shadow almost against his will. The house, I told Sam, has to do with childhood. To children, doors are a lot larger than they are to us, to us grownups. Time is much bigger to them than to us. A day can feel like a month. A door can feel like a cavern, and overhead a great emptiness of space hangs like the presence of fear. Sam at once saw the point."

"Of course," Emerson said. "I knew *he* would see."

"Why, yes," I said, vaguely irritated by his attitude. "He got the point right away."

"So now you can go ahead with collecting things for this house from your mother?"

"I started yesterday." I felt triumphant.

"Your mother is selling you these objects you want at a reduction, I assume. She is taking into consideration you are her son."

"That wouldn't be fair," I said. "I pay her just like anyone else. She has to make a living like anyone else. I can afford to pay twice the price she asks for anyway."

"Your mother is a good businesswoman, an admirably self-reliant person. I see that."

What was he driving at?

"My mother has always stressed that she can take care of herself, that I learn to take care of myself, which I've done. Why should either of us go back on our values?" I am an upright Yankee. Did I have to point this out to him? I come from a high-minded background. I believe in hard work, no self-indulgence, paying my way, incurring no debts.

"Considering that your mother was the wife of a professional man, a doctor, why all this stress on taking care of herself?"

"Dad was idealistic, impractical. He never asked anyone who seemed hard up to pay his bills. That made her furious—I mean, that made her more practical than she might otherwise have been. It was an adjustment, let's say, to the facts of her life. She admired my father deeply. He is so selfless, she used to say. They loved each other . . ." I remembered how I felt the last time we touched on this subject. I could not go on.

"You can afford to pay twice the price, you just said," he prompted me.

"I didn't say I'd pay twice the price. I don't require that much of myself. But if she overcharged me—I don't say she does—but if she overcharged me, I, yes, I would pay it if she asked me to. She is my mother. She needs to make a living. She's got to be independent. It's important to her."

"If you could get the exact same chair at another antiques store at half the price your mother charges, would you go to the other store?"

I thought about it. Felt it out. "I don't think so. She needs to make a living."

"Isn't it interesting that you decorate your dreams (your work, your scenes, your creations are your waking dreams) with things you get from your mother?" You see how well he understands metaphors!

"I buy a lot of props from other places."

"But only after checking that your mother doesn't have the same things."

"That's right. But she is in the antiques business. I have to stress she has to earn a living."

"I gather she does all right."

"She's quite successful, more than just solvent. She has worked up a pretty good portfolio of stocks for herself. She lives nicely in an apartment in a mews and has a good social life. She takes a long trip or a cruise once a year."

"In other words, you do not need to be a faithful customer in order to keep her afloat financially."

"Maybe not." He'd thrown me directly up against this reflection I saw of myself. I *wanted* to shop in my mother's store. I wanted to buy things from her that I could get elsewhere. I wanted to buy from her.

I said suspiciously, "You think I want to keep a connection with her?"

Ah . . . he seemed to say.

"Well, she is my mother. The only one I'll ever have." I laughed, but my laughter sounded unhappy to my ears.

Ah . . . he seemed to say again.

"No matter what I do or don't do, she's the only one I'll ever have. No one else in the whole world is my mother. She's it. What can I do?"

"Keep buying, I suppose," he said offhandedly.

His attitude seemed callous. I would never have imagined I could find him callous.

"What does to buy mean to you?" he asked.

Here we go again, I thought. "To buy," I said obediently, "is to give money in exchange for goods. I give her a check for two hundred dollars and she gives me a colonial bureau or something."

"You give first, then she gives you something in turn."

"I give first?" He was right. My idea of buying was to take out my wallet and then receive the article. To some people the order was reversed: you received the article and then took out your checkbook to pay the bill.

"You buy an awful lot," he said. "From your mother."

Words are interesting. The overuse of a word cancels out its meaning. Or, conversely, its use in another turn of phrase gives it an allegorical meaning.

"To buy," I said, "also means to accept another person's idea of something, or of himself. To buy his notion of the truth, say. I buy my mother." I repeated to myself, I buy my mother.

I no longer shook these days. I found myself trembling. To shake is to be shaky, to suffer from a fear of loss of control. When I was shaky, my knees often felt as if they were about to buckle. I felt helpless, weak. But when I started to tremble, I was trembling as with the expectation of joy. I trembled at odd times, at work, at home, in a cab, talking to Sam. Especially talking to Sam about my project. I felt faint when I shook but rigid when I trembled.

I didn't tell Emerson that I myself couldn't buy some of this psychoanalytic bit. (He would only have rejoined that I was resisting.) Some of the "solutions" seemed just too pat, too obvious, too quid pro quo. I suppose he, the trained psychiatrist, wouldn't have bought that. Though skeptical, I at the same time figured out to my own satisfaction that my wife Edith's guiltiness is the direct result of being the eldest of six children. It's that pat. She got pushed aside as each child was born; she turned her anger over loss into "love," and against herself. She learned the lesson too well that she must make way for others, others she must not hate but must protect. No wonder she arms herself to the teeth for others; braced with arguments from liberal magazines, she defends the more helpless around the world, tooth and nail. But she leaves herself unprotected from her own self-doubt. As the eldest child, everything was expected of her at too young an age. It *is* so obvious. It boggles my mind. I determined to get that baby nurse for her. I would explain to my wife why she, Edith, deserved the best herself.

Had her only choice always been either to deny herself and fight for the demanding but weaker ones who usurped her place one by one (and thereby to reap approval and self-esteem) or, as Edith did not do, to turn cool, to withdraw, to keep herself to herself as much as possible? But Edith is not a selfish person. I love her, sought her, because she is not a selfish person. I told Dr. Emerson this.

"It was important to you not to marry a selfish person?"

"I admire unselfish people," I said. "I admire people who put themselves out for others."

"You put yourself out for that Nan person, didn't you?"

"My mother said when I was young, 'If you really loved your father, as I do, you wouldn't think about yourself so much.' You see," I told Emerson, "my father was a completely giving man. He was this small-town doctor, running himself ragged taking care of the sick all day, most evenings and weekends. He was always busy. I rarely saw him.

"My mother was on her own. She rarely saw him too, so she had to be self-reliant, unselfish about the situation and fill up her time the best she could. I used to hang on to him for dear life when he was home, to make up for when he was absent. He and I were very close. It was all very intense. If it was appropriate to, he used to take me with him on some of his calls. I suppose I must have been eight or nine when he did that. I remember him from those days better than I do from later days. He died of a heart attack when I was twenty-five. I thought it ironic that it should be a heart attack. He had so much heart, you wouldn't think he'd have worn it out."

"You were an only child, I assume. You have never told me."

"Oh yes. I was always alone."

"Really?" he said, as if surprised.

"An only child is alone a lot. And given my parents, I suppose I was alone more than most."

"Alone in a big house?"

"My mother stopped me from clinging to my father when he had to go. She said I was being selfish to keep him from sick people. 'Do you see me keeping your father from his work?' I can hear her saying. She was right, of course. I had to try to be grown up about it, the way she was grown up about it. She is a woman of enormous inner resources," I said.

"Did your mother always have an antiques store to keep herself busy?"

I shook my head. Something was wrong with the way he put that question. She had never done anything just to keep busy. She always knew what she wanted to do. Had I given him the idea she dabbled in antiques simply to have something to busy herself with?

I said, "My mother was an actress. This antiques store business is something relatively new. My mother was a very beautiful woman. She was an actress before she got married, and she still acted, mostly in summer stock, when I was quite young. Through acting and later having something to do with props, she got interested in antiques. Around the time my father died, she had a friend in whose store she helped out, and eventually she became this friend's partner. To make a long story short, she bought out the friend three years ago and owns this place herself now. She is a very smart businesswoman, as you pointed out."

"You have some of your mother's acumen and some of her talent," he said. Often he said things just to see how I'd react to them, obvious things that did not manifest his perspicacity so much as his skill. It was a ploy of his to act quite dense on occasion.

I said nothing. I must have had a peculiar expression on my face.

"Are you angry with me?" he asked.

"I look angry?" I rearranged my face. Now I assumed I looked blandly daft.

"You resent my linking your mother's abilities with your own. But you deliberately build your art works with material taken from your mother's store. You build scenes, as in plays, and your mother turns out to have been an actress. You have taken from your mother's past and her present to make a place for yourself in life. I am forced to conclude you are trying to act out something."

That was the understatement of the year. At that session I simply retorted, "I was an artist long before I developed this new genre of mine. What did color field have to do with my mother's turn-of-the-century junk?" I was not buying some of Emerson's bridges to my past, to the experience that formed me.

I did not tell him I was holding back on some information, not from the past, but about developments that had been taking place in the present.

I had had the feeling that Nan Weil was softening toward me. I had a feeling she was no longer avoiding me. Could it be her work was going so well she could look up from it and take time out to be civil? Perhaps she missed having me breathing down her pretty neck.

She had stuck her head in the door one day and said, "Hi, stranger. How's everything?"

"Hi," I answered, dumfounded.

"So long." She smiled.

That was all. But she needn't have put her head in the door at all. Now, now, I said to myself, you are making a whole loaf out of a single miserable crumb. Don't be a fool.

I was not a fool, and I kept out of her way. But I was anxious anyway, trying at the same time to get Sam Dexter's okay on the size of the door for my new *oeuvre,* and being worried about Edith. She was having a little difficulty with her pregnancy. Her doctor had ordered her to bed for a week. I did not mention either Edith or this brief exchange with Nan to Emerson. What was there to mention?

Bob Meacham had been plaguing us to think about going to Europe in the spring when he would be there. After he wound up his seminars and poetry workshop the first week of January, he was going up to the art colony for a couple of months to work on his third book of poems. Then he was taking off for six months in France—this sabbatical was what he lived for. I told him over long distance phone that we were expecting a child at the end of April so it was no dice. He said he'd be in Provence March first. We should stay with him until the middle of April, and then fly home for the birth. I told him he knew nothing about pregnancy. He retorted that he had a child, remember. I said airlines did not take pregnant women the last few weeks of their pregnancies. I must admit I felt rather resentful that this unborn infant's schedule was in the way of a perfect vacation. Bob Meacham knew the ropes in Provence. He knew the ropes about a lot of things—women, southern French landscape, keeping house without a refrigerator in a foreign hamlet.

Nan brought me a container of coffee one day. She waltzed into my office and said, "You work too hard," and handed me the coffee. She walked over to Miss Price and handed her a container too. I now had two new permanent full-time men working at the far end of the loft. She looked at them and said to me, "Pretty soon you'll have a factory turning these things out and then you'll be absolutely unapproachable." She has a fine sense of humor. Me, unapproachable! I felt all turned around. I had pulled a Bob Meacham on her—inadvertently —by keeping out of her way.

I ran into her in the stationery store one day. She asked me to hold something for her while she dug in her bag for money. We walked back together to 269 East Fifty-fourth Street. She said, "Time has always been biting at my heels, so to speak. I never had much time to do anything for myself, so I've been kind of making up for it by cutting back on everything else. My husband understands it so well. He says I'm acting out something that I always had to deny myself. That's why I'm so excited to be working on this novel. It is all about time and what time means to people. Time is blood. Blood in an hour-glass, leaking away."

My head swam. Nan Weil had never talked that much to me before. She was telling me about herself. And what she was telling me proved she was a woman of enormous sensibility. I watched her climb up to her floor. I worshiped the ground she walked on. I was hooked again.

How could I tell Emerson? I'd promised him—no, I'd promised myself—that I was through with Nan. Somewhere in the back of my superstitious Sunday-school religious mind I was under the impression he took me back under his wing because I said I'd made such progress, so much progress that I was through with Nan. I didn't want to disappoint him. I didn't want him to know.

It suddenly dawned on me Nan was apologizing for her former curtness. She was explaining why she had not had the time of day for me. I was flooded with gratitude and a sense of well-being.

It was almost Christmas. How fast time goes for adults. How slowly for Amanda. Amanda had been waiting for Christmas since July. I had designed a party package then in which the napkins were large folded snowflakes. It was Amanda's favorite package, and now Nan, seeing some in my office, bought one, I assumed for her children. Now

I again believed she had children. I believed again she was married. As I say, belief itself is my problem. I really don't know what to believe. Am I an artist because of my early experience? Was my experience truly what I remembered it as being? Or did it only seem like that to me? I have wrested profit from this doubt of myself. Reality seems too real to me, and also not real enough. I have to make art to mirror this reality, art which joins this reality as a new contribution to it. It is my way of staking myself in reality. I produce, therefore I am.

Nan asked me to look into her office one day. She was on her way down when she put her head in the door and said, "If you can spare ten minutes later, say in half an hour, I'd like to show you something."

Miss Price said, as Nan's head disappeared, "Maybe she did buy herself a stapler, after all. Maybe she wants to show you a stapler." The kind of information about a person that stays in Miss Price's head is truly unbelievable. Nan had borrowed the use of our stapler once, more than a year ago.

I went up two minutes after I saw her return. I knocked on the door. She said, "Come in, it's open," and I entered. Why was every bit of this so delicious to me? She put down a pencil and turned around. She waved me to her sling chair and then went to a thermos and poured out some cold juice and handed me a paper cup of it.

"I just thought," she said, "you should see my office once anyway. After all, you're responsible for how it looks. I never did thank you for the paint job."

"You never asked me for it either," I said, feeling quite in command of myself.

She laughed. I drank her in with the apple juice.

"I simply had to show someone what I've done." She lifted some bulging folders and brought them to me.

"Your novel?"

"That's the first draft. My ex-novel, I call it. That eight hundred pages is just a first draft. It took me two years to write. I have put it all aside. This writing business is killing." Brimming over with joy, she skipped back to the deal table. My poster was over her bed where I'd put it.

She picked up the bottom of a box, the kind that holds typing paper, and lifted an inch of paper to show me. "That's the first third of my novel, eight chapters in all. I just got it back from my editor. My editor's name is Amos Harding. Isn't that a terrific name? Amos Harding. He's the most sensitive, perceptive, understanding man in New York, except for my husband, of course. My agent is arranging the details of my contract. I'm going to be a real live novelist. Can you believe it?"

"I love you," I said. I love you despairingly.

"I love it," she said, hugging the eight chapters. "I'm absolutely crazy with joy about it all. All my life I've wanted to be a writer and now I'm a writer." Her eyes grew big and frightened. She went back to the deal table and clutched the top of it. The party package she'd bought from Miss Price was on the table. So she had not yet taken it home.

"Are you all right!" I exclaimed, going up to her. She behaved as if she were in the throes of a heart attack.

"I'm just touching wood," she said. "I've been a fool to tell you all this. It'll jinx everything, I won't be able to write another line, and then I'm a goner. Just forget everything I've said. Just put it right out of your mind." She was still clinging to the table.

"Good thing it's not formica," I said.

She didn't laugh. She was counting to twenty or something. When she felt she'd touched wood long enough, she relaxed a little but did not smile. The gods might punish levity. "You see, until I got married, I had to work to help support someone in the family. I never made much, I'm not saying I did. But half of my salary as a secretary went to the care of this invalid uncle. It didn't leave enough for me, for my mother and me, to live decently. So I had odd jobs evenings, like manuscript typing, or helping out in stores weekends, that kind of thing. I moonlighted through college and for five years after that. I figured I put in a seventy-five-hour week usually. I was able to get a poem done now and then. But a novel is such a big project. You really have to have time to let go, really sink into it. My husband understands, and wants me to take all the time I need to write this novel. To see if I have it in me, and to go on if I do. I really am so lucky. He says I'm making up for lost time, and finding myself. So I'm really doing two things at once. I'm writing. And I'm evolving as a person. My life is going on at two levels because of being able to do what I really want to do. *You* know what it is to be able to do what you want to do. You must appreciate your life so much, I know you must, your painting or whatever you call it."

I was mesmerized. I don't really remember what I answered.

"Sometimes I'm so happy I'm scared stiff," she said, throwing out her arms and squeezing herself.

"You are beautiful."

"So are you!" she said, flinging her arms out to the room, to the world.

I was standing right next to her. I was a man, after all. Anxious, desperate, unsure, but I was a full-blooded man even then. I said, "I'm trying to get something across to you. I have been for months. I love you. I love you for everything you are."

Nan Weil heard me. What she heard surprised her. I suppose she had never realized that what I had done in my erratic fashion had been an expression of love. She hadn't seen. But, I swear, I thought in the last couple of months she had missed having me in her hair. Women do need to be pursued, whether they'll admit it or not.

"I love you more than I can say."

"Oh, you mustn't," she said. Her behavior has always been perfect. With me, that is.

She didn't say, You are mad, go away, or I can't have that, or It's too ridiculous.

She said, "Oh, you mustn't," meaning, It is best that you do not. You mustn't hurt yourself. You must not be in love with me, because *I* do not want you to be hurt. It was a declaration of affection. That's what I saw.

I took it that she was not repelled by the idea of my being in love with her. She doesn't have the remotest suggestion of a hard streak in her. She was opening up, opened up, by the fact that she was writing well, that she was doing what she had apparently waited years to do. She was tender, alive, fertile to new experience. That was my interpretation. I have not been proven to be wrong.

"I've been watching you for almost a year," I said. Actually, it was a year and a half, but I was embarrassed to admit it.

She looked at me and past me. I suddenly had the feeling that she'd had a circumscribed girlhood. (Her mother was separated from her father. Her uncle, the invalid, had stayed with them until his long hospitalization and death.) Having lived the middle-class life of a Jewish girl without means, she probably had not had too much sexual or even social experience.

She'd met her husband one summer when finally she'd been able to save enough money to take a vacation. She was twenty-four then, and they'd gone together for two years before marrying five years ago. She'd actually had to live at home until she was twenty-five.

I saw the whole picture, and was torn between my desire for her and my feeling that she needed to be protected from any possible experience with me. In other words, I was just beginning to see her for what she actually was. Not the foreign princess, self-possessed, remote, in full charge of herself. She was Nan Weil, a lovely girl, and a thirty-one-year-old woman who was learning to write as she wrote a novel.

"I'm not looking for trouble," she said gravely. "You shouldn't be either," referring to my wife and child. "What I need most of all is to be a writer."

She is so real, so unconfused, so candid, so on the level. "Most of all" she needed to be a writer. But also? But what else did she need? World, world, how we each create what we need, for better or for worse. Be careful what you wish for, for in middle age you will find your wishes have come true.

I think Edith's miscarriage had something to do with it. She lost the baby a couple of weeks after my conversation with Nan. To lose a child, even a fetus, feels like a refusal to be creative, a refusal to invent. We do invent our own children, don't we? The unborn or the miscarried cancel out possibilities—never undertaken—never aired in the light of the world.

Edith slept for three days afterward. I cared for her at home, but I also felt released from a vow. I do not like myself now for it.

I knocked on Nan's door.

She let me in, as if she had been expecting me. It was snowing outside, the whiteness closing us in with that meaningfulness an ordinary fall of snow communicates, each flake an unspoken word. Snow makes any day like Sunday, personal, intimate, a hiatus foreboding nothing evil, nothing good. Simply, existence is confirmed: here and now. Snow is not transcendent. It fills the world, breaches the void, reaches the child in us, and says, Give up the struggle, forget aspiration, be. Be, and I will return you to the absolute center of the present moment.

She heated some water on the burner on the windowsill. The steam on the window cut us off from the world—we were in our own snug household. I sat down on her bed under my poster. She joined me. We drank instant tea. I knew what she was thinking. She knew what I was thinking.

I got up and locked her door. When I sat down again, she said in a loud voice, "I love Herb."

I said, softer, "I love Edith."

I did not like myself for saying it. It is a way of declaring you want to eat your cake and have it too; dishonestly, it pretends to honesty. The way she said, "I love Herb," was different. I think she meant, Am I losing my bearings? I love my husband and here I am sitting here expecting what? Expecting anything. What is happening to me?

After all, the whole idea of wanting me, if she wanted me at all, was newer to her than my idea of wanting her. I'd wanted her since my childhood, I gather.

I kissed her. The way she responded I knew she had some feeling for me. She stood up and slowly went to the door. I followed and kissed her at the door. I kissed her for a full ten minutes, I think. At the door she was much more relaxed than on the bed. She was so fresh, so young, so responsive. Finally we stopped. With her hand behind me, she unlocked the door. She said nothing.

Had she been less serious, less solemn, we would have gone much further that time. Laughter can dispel the earnestness that is a part of passion, and too much graveness is more than sexuality can survive. I realized this was just the beginning; our moment was yet to come. We were passing through the religious ceremony into the secular; the carnal would follow after that.

Now we were more than friends, of course, and I felt as if I were emerging from a dream into actuality.

At Dr. Emerson's we were working on my early childhood, I was going to say. Truthfully, however, I was still fearful of yielding up my beginnings. Every life is a story. Life itself is fictitious in feeling, perhaps in fact, always in its unreal reality or its real unreality. Life is schizoid in feeling. I feel this even now, and I am well. I was afraid to lose myself in self-discovery. Afraid that to surrender my sickness might also be to forfeit my positive drive, my creative force. To cure myself might change me in ways that would be a kind of suicide, or so it seemed to me. To change the self is to risk dying. To take that risk, that gamble of the ego, is fearsome and appears self-destructive. How much easier to endure oneself as one has been for just another thirty-seven years. Why not shake a little, suffer a little nausea, feel deprived? I was used to these feelings. I could handle them in my way. Right after Nan had put her head in the door and said, "Hi, stranger," I'd gone back to the tranquilizers I'd been taking before I'd returned to Dr. Emerson, just an average dose.

I was telling Dr. Emerson that I'd found my mother strangely reluctant to sell me several things I needed for my "house," which I had named by now. It was to be called "Love," simply love. He found it profoundly interesting that an empty house should be called "Love." I said my titles had all been rather prosaic: "The Porch," with its sand sifting endlessly; "The Bachelor," an arrangement of bones on a double bed; "The Nursery," which is in the museum in Boston, an assemblage of three papier-mâché arms with incomplete hands suspended over a crib. This was the first time, I explained, I was using an oblique title, an ironic one.

"Pris is holding back on a dining set and hooked rugs I need for the floors."

"Pris?"

"My mother. I've called her Pris for years. Short for Priscilla. She always wanted to be something on her own, not just Mom."

"How do you feel about this reluctance of hers?"

"Surprisingly irritated." I suppose my face indicated more than irritation.

"Simply irritated?"

"Angry."

"Why is she holding back on you?"

I had to clear my throat several times before I could speak. I was breathing heavily. I suppose I really was furious. "I don't know."

"Did you ask her?"

"No."

"You got good results when you told Sam why the door of 'Love' had to be oversize. Why don't you ask your mother why she is reluctant to part with the dining set?"

It was a good idea. I resolved to ask her next Sunday when I went down to the Village. She wanted me to move some things for her; she was making room for new items that were due to come in the following week.

Meanwhile, we spoke of love. "Puttykins surprised us recently," I told Emerson. "Edith was still in bed because of her miscarriage. I was reading in the bedroom to keep her company. Puttykins was playing mother with her doll on our bed. She shook her doll and said, 'I'll love you if you're good. You be good, or Mommy won't love you.' She shook the doll violently by its neck. It is a brand-new doll and cost a lot.

111

" 'Hey!' I exclaimed, looking up from *Art News*.

" 'It's a bargaining world,' Edith said to me, raising her eyebrows. She addressed herself to Amanda. 'You must love her *into* being good.' This was over Amanda's head, of course.

" 'If I eat my vegble,' Amanda said, 'can I take her head off?'

" 'She's making another bargain!' I said to Edith.

" 'If you eat your vegetables, not vegbles, you'll grow up to be a big girl. You are making an incorrect syllogism. Eating or not eating your carrots has nothing to do with how you treat your doll,' Edith said. She believes in not talking down to children.

" 'Why do you want to take her head off?' I asked my daughter.

" 'I have to see,' she said.

" 'See what?'

" 'See if she's good inside, if she's really good.'

" 'Will you be able to tell?'

" 'Course. You could too.'

"Nothing more was exchanged, but Edith and I thought perhaps we should make more of an effort to widen her social life. The two kids she played with might be cynical monsters."

"You think what she said was monstrous?" Dr. Emerson asked.

"She didn't know what she was saying. She's three. But goodness and love preclude," I said, finding out what I wanted to say as I said it, "the sort of intensive examination she was going to put her doll through. By bargaining about love she is denying love."

"Love to be love must be blind," Dr. Emerson said.

"Yes," I said to the obvious.

"That is your problem," he said.

"God!" I cried. "My problem is some kind of shapeless octopus. It's all over the place. Love is my problem, seeing is my problem, believing is my problem, anxiety is my problem, my 'house' is my problem!"

He seemed to nod.

I was on the verge. But since my problem was tied up with my self, and since wanting to survive seemed more urgent than wanting to live (relaxedly), I did not see what I was on the verge of.

The next time I saw Emerson, he said, "Did you ask your mother?"

"It was very difficult," I said.

"She was busy?"

"*I* found it difficult to bring up. But I'm spending all this time and money getting myself straightened out, so I was determined." I was saying to him, I'm no shirker. "I did it indirectly," I admitted somewhat shamefacedly. "I took out my checkbook and said, 'As long as I'm making out a check for the kitchen stuff, why don't I just add in the cost of the dining set and the rugs?' I watched her face carefully. I am a watcher."

"And . . . ?" Dr. Emerson prompted me.

"She opened her eyes wide, glared at me and said, 'I am not selling you the dining things or the rugs, now that's the end of the matter.'

" 'But Pris,' I pleaded, 'I'm paying you for them.'

"My mother has becoming gray hair, done in a youthful over-one-eye style; she's a little overweight but still femininely attractive; and she dresses like a suburban lady who might have a swimming pool and give a dance on the terrace once a year. I have never understood why she hasn't got remarried. She has beaus. 'I would not desecrate the memory of your father by marrying again,' she has said.

"I was pulling out a bureau for her, making space for the new shipment. She sighed. 'You never move things out far enough,' she said. 'Move those things over here right now while I'm watching. When the men deliver tomorrow, they'll need to get back in there. And don't forget the thing in the basement has to be fixed.'

"You don't love me at all, I wanted to say."

"What did she say to that?" Dr. Emerson asked.

"I only thought that; I didn't say it. It's too childish, and not true anyway. I said, 'The dining set has a sentimental value, I suppose.'

"She laughed quite histrionically. After all, she was an actress once. 'I can get a terrific price for it from some fool who buys for an out-of-town outfit. Why should I let it go to you at a reasonable price?'

"You see," I said to Emerson, "she didn't want to hold me up on the price."

"And this proves what?"

"That she cares for me."

"Had you told her how much you needed the things for your work?"

"Why, sure."

"You told her they were just what you needed?"

I nodded.

"She's not desperate for money," he said, "but as long as she knows she can get more for them from someone else, she is denying them to you on the rationale that she can't overcharge you, her son. She is being fair, but she is also being a good businesswoman."

"Exactly."

"But how did you feel about it? Not think, but *feel* about it?"

I closed my eyes, pretending I had to work hard at putting myself back in her store two days before, but I knew exactly how I felt. I was distressed, ashamed to feel what I felt. I was wrong to feel the way I felt. But I decided I must let him know the depths of my wrongness, my twisted nature. I was paying him to tell him the absolute shameful facts.

"I hate her!" I said. My hands shook. "That's the awful truth. I hate her guts. I was so angry. Angry. Can you believe it? Now *that* really is my problem, isn't it? Being so angry. What right had I to be angry? She's just being a good businesswoman. She loves me."

"You confuse your wanting, needing, her love with what she gives you. Your need is great, *was* great, not her love."

"She gives me a pain," I said bitterly, enraged.

"You have always buried your anger," he said. "From the beginning of time."

"I have too much anger in me. I want to get rid of it."

"That is correct. You must express it."

"Express it?" That idea was brand-new. Revolutionary.

"*You* have to learn to express it. With some people it comes naturally."

"Express it," I repeated. But it felt right; it almost cleared my head.

114

I pushed on at once. "With whom? With Miss Price?"

"With your mother," he said.

"With my mother!"

But he couldn't mean what he was saying; it was impossible. I was stunned, exhausted, thinking, but on the return flow of advancing thought. I sat shocked for several long minutes. As with a problem in a painting, a speck of content made all sorts of variations, of details, fall into place.

My mother (where I am involved) is a phony. Pris is not selfless, she is selfish. Pris and Dad did not get along; they rubbed each other the wrong way—they suffered with each other and called it love. My mother has not married again because she is threatened by other people's needs. My mother hasn't much to give. She takes, but she calls it giving. She is afraid, in fact, of being taken. My father had never been able to cope with her, so he escaped into overwork, and he was admired for the overwork and so forgave himself for his ineffectualness. My father had bought a whole bag of tricks from my mother. He had been duped, as I was duped. My mother had wanted a life of her own from the very beginning, so she married a man whose personality and whose profession would leave her as much time as she needed for herself. She was shrewder than he. He was a victim of his own delusions. He had not been very bright where love was concerned. A good general practitioner can be backward in areas outside his work.

I cannot say all this came to me that day, but everything I realized was realized all at the same time. It took two or three sessions for me to sort it all out. I had, indeed, bought more than I thought from my mother.

"But they were human," I said. "My parents had to go after what they needed, make the adjustments they had to make, given the kind of people they were, live their lives."

"Of course," he said. "That is not in question. You came to me because of *your* feelings of despair over that Nan person."

"I simply can't believe my new view of . . . of all that history. I can't believe my mother's idea of her marriage is incorrect." I remember wincing, my eyes closing against all they saw.

"To you it is a fraud. She is a phony, you said."

"I can't believe my father was not what he thought he was, the selfless doctor making his rounds eighteen hours a day. Actually, he was escaping responsibility to himself in other areas by working compulsively. Imagine."

"What does selflessness mean to you?"

We had been tacking back and forth over these questions for months now. Each time, as on a spiral, I came back to the same point, but I came back at a different level.

"Without a self. Weak," I said.

"And selfishness?"

"Weak, unsure, hanging on to self by blocking out other people's needs, real or imaginary demands. Keeping oneself to oneself." I laughed bitterly. "It's no good to be either selfish *or* unselfish. It's all weakness, one way or another. You simply can't win."

"Do you really believe that?"

"I'm the one who never is sure what to believe."

"The self that is strong is self-assertive but relaxed, considerate of others but not withdrawn, free and therefore responsible, creative and appropriately giving." Those were not quite his words and perhaps he did not say them just then. Perhaps this is just my own understanding of maturity—for which he is responsible.

"I had a dream," I said.

"A waking dream?"

"No. A sleeping dream. At last."

"Congratulations," he said and folded his hands together to listen.

"I dreamed I was looking into my mother's head to see if she really was good. Actually, it was Amanda with her doll which gave me the idea, so it's not really much of a dream."

"Was that all there was to it?"

"Then the head somehow became my head. I was looking into my own head, noticing it had walls, which surprised me, walls like a room. The walls defined my area of . . . of possession. My bodily territory. Yet I—looking in on me—was bodiless."

"What was in your head?"

"Lots of things. It was chock full of things—but I was out. I was not in, not at home. Dreams are really insane."

"How did you feel about discovering you were out?"

"I was terrified, and full of disbelief. I suppose I really don't believe in myself," I said. "I don't really believe in my own existence. That's my interpretation for today."

"I suggest," he said later, apropos of something else, "that you assert yourself with your mother the next time she says something you don't quite buy."

"I must express my anger," I said, nervous about the whole enterprise.

"Appropriate anger must be expressed," he said. "Not what you think but what you *feel* must be expressed." I felt alarmed, but I had to admit tentatively, even secretively to myself, I see. I see.

I was almost at the end of my education, my formal twice-a-week schooling, though I suppose the rest of my life will be a learning process, a further exploration of what Dr. Emerson has helped me to see.

I had still not told him about seeing Nan again. It was right after Christmas, and a new snowfall, covering the sodden, grimy leavings of that earlier snow, had disguised everything with a fraudulent, glistening cosmetic. I could not stay away. I went up to Nan's office to give her a bottle of perfume, a present for Christmas, wrapped in gold paper and tied with tinsel. It was an extravagant gift, almost a hundred dollars' worth of a perfume called "Longing."

"I really can't accept that from you," she said, holding me with her eyes, saying, I don't want to hurt you, but I really mustn't accept it, and you must understand I am not rejecting you, just the perfume. She put the perfume on the deal table; she still hadn't taken home the party package she'd bought. That bothered me.

"You've accepted more than that from me already," I said, pressing toward her.

"I have?" She wondered what I meant.

"You have accepted that I love you." I knew this was true.

"George, I do like you. I think I even care for you a little. But—"

"You accepted my poster and my fixing up this place."

"I could hardly scrape off the paint," she said without a smile. She was deliciously serious.

"There is nothing so committing about some perfume."

"Not to me. But maybe it means something to you."

"Of course it means something to me!" I exclaimed. "To me. Who else? To me. Me! Me! Me!"

She looked at me strangely, and tactfully, not wanting to upset me further, moved away, as if to pick up a pencil or a book.

I went for her then. I pulled her to me—her back was turned—and swung her around forcibly. I kissed her furiously. Roughly, vengefully, furiously. I dragged her, as she tried to disentangle herself and take a breath, toward the bed. I pushed her onto the bed and began to kiss her and to try to get rid of her dress at the same time. I was full of hate.

"Let go!" she cried. "Are you off your rocker!" She had said this to me once before, hadn't she?

"I love you," I said, in a rage.

She tore herself away in one stupendous lunge. "You don't look as if you love me at all!" she retorted with a kind of angry dismay. I went for her again, roughly. She slapped me hard. I had hurt her; I had disappointed her. She's no fool. She saw what she saw and believed in her own reaction. "You are hateful!"

Red in the face, breathing hard, I pulled myself together. I was humiliated, disgraced. I had been about to do violence to my Nan. I felt both weak and strong. I felt out of control. I was afraid *of* myself.

She went to the door, pulled down her dress with an angry yank, and opened the door.

"You don't love me at all!" she said, practically in tears. "I thought you loved me!"

I was so confused I ran downstairs without looking at her and stayed at a corner table in the delicatessen the rest of the afternoon. I drank a lot of beer and buried my face in my hands on the table, as if drunk. When I got back to my office the perfume was on my desk.

I had to tell Dr. Emerson now. I, the amorous fool who had discovered things about himself, was now turning into a would-be rapist. But it wasn't at all funny. It was potentially dangerous and filled me with horror.

I told him everything: how—at her initiative—I had started seeing Nan again. And how I felt she had begun to care for me.

He said sharply at that point, "You withheld this from me too long."

I hurried on to make up for my delay and told him about the time of the first snowfall and then about what happened just the day before. I did not spare myself the details. "Thank heaven, she stopped me!" I cried. Ah yes, thank heaven, indeed. Dr. Emerson thanked heaven too.

Dr. Emerson closed his eyes (his contact lenses sometimes bothered him) and sighed very loudly. He looked to the right and to the left, like a man following a tennis ball. He squeezed his eyes closed again. He'd never behaved like this before, and I'd made quite a study of him.

"You don't believe me, do you?" I asked. Perhaps he thought I was exaggerating my overassertive behavior. Perhaps he could not believe I, George Safford, was no longer the humble lover, too happy with crumbs.

"I believe you," he said grimly.

"I really did make myself felt," I said.

He struggled with himself. He sighed deeply again. He finally pulled himself together. He then sat looking directly at me, instead of swinging his head in the narrow arc. He looked at me with an unfamiliar combination of wariness, disbelief, and self-contempt. No, not self-contempt, but an exasperated ruefulness. I didn't understand this change in him. I looked at him, bewildered; I decided I must be wrong; I was reading it all wrong. And I suppose, since he knew what he was doing, he saw me going through my usual syndrome of perceptions (based on my sensibilities) and my scuttling of them, because I found it difficult to believe what I perceived. He told me much later that he decided then and there—it was a calculated risk—he had to act decisively in this mixed-up case. He had to force me to learn to believe in myself. He used me as a learning aid. He used me against myself. For myself.

"What did you say she called her husband?" he asked me, apropos of nothing. His eyes seemed bloodshot with some kind of repressed emotion. It looked like horror to me.

"Herb." What had that got to do with anything?

We skipped around a lot.

"You mistake this Nan person," he said, "for your mother."

"So that's why I seemed to be furious!"

"That's why you *were* furious."

It was a minor revelation that I mistook Nan for Pris. The idea repelled me, but I felt I could accept it, for I had actually been hateful to Nan. I had not been loving to this mother figure.

He next got me around to Nan's novel. He seemed to know an awful lot about it, but I had reported to him word for word what she had told me, and he did have a retentive memory. Still, how did he know that her editor, Amos Harding, was an ex-musician who'd gone into publishing when he was forty-five. As a musician, he had a special understanding of her subject and method: time. She had never told me any of this, so I could not have relayed it to him. I was puzzled too simply because he spent the rest of that session on Nan's work. But I had a lot of other things on my mind, such as that Nan was leaving for the art colony (she'd told me this breathlessly a week ago in the hall), and now I was wondering what to do about saying good-by to her. Should I just pretend the other day had not happened? Or should I let her go without saying good-by? When she returned a month later (she was only spending January up in Vermont), she might even have forgotten all about the unfortunate incident. It was the day before New Year's Eve that I was back at Dr. Emerson's.

He was quite brisk, friendly, inclined to chat a bit.

"Are you planning to celebrate tomorrow evening?" he asked.

Sometimes we did go in for a bit of social exchange, just a little, for I didn't want my money to go down the drain of small talk.

"We're throwing a party at the office. I'm stringing up some lanterns and things. Edith is wearing her new silver gown. Someone is setting up a hi-fi. It promises to be a blast." I suddenly thought, Maybe he is hinting he would like to come. Did one's psychiatrist mix with one socially? "Perhaps you and your wife could drop by," I said.

He caught himself on an inhalation of air. He cleared his throat. "Thank you," he said. "We are already engaged for the evening. And my wife has to be on the way to Vermont the next day."

"Well, some other time," I said.

"My wife is going to spend the month of January up there doing her work," he said. "The whole month of January."

This was the first time I was given a glimpse into his life. I hadn't even known he had a wife. I'd assumed he had, but he had never mentioned any aspect of his life to me before. Did this mean he thought I was pretty close to being discharged as cured? Was I being gently let loose into the world not as a patient but as a confidant, an intimate, of his?

He continued: "My wife is going up there to work on a project without any interruptions. She could take two months. In fact, I've tried to persuade her to take two months, but she is a conscientious wife and doesn't want to leave me at loose ends for that long."

"Edith would be just like that."

"Our wives have something in common," he said. "They are both quite unspoiled."

I felt very happy at this display of his generosity, his relating my life to his.

"What is your wife's name?" I asked.

He hesitated. "With me, she goes by the name of Annette."

I laughed. With him, she went by the name of Annette. "With the radio repairman, she is Mrs. Emerson, of course," I said.

He smiled. "We are attracted to the same kind of woman, I suspect," he said, making us buddies. How incredible the whole psychoanalytic process was turning out to be! I felt very happy, but I was also tensed up, ready for anything.

"Well, you would know better than I," I said, meaning that he knew me. I didn't know him as well.

"I'm in a position to know it only too well," he said.

Enough of this socializing, I thought. Being at the analyst's is like being in a cab with the meter going. Every ticking moment is expensive, really expensive. I am a Calvinist, and while I'll buy Edith a deepfreeze or a second car, I don't like to see money wasting to no purpose.

I said firmly, directing the conversation, "I am already looking forward to spring, when I start assembling 'Love.' I am beginning to understand it—the house. I am beginning to see all of it." I looked eagerly into his face. He returned the look. "I am beginning to believe that I knew all along the unreal quality of my parents' love—for me and for each other. If, when I was young, I didn't believe what I felt, it was because I was afraid to believe what I felt. If I believed they did not love me (which the evidence pointed to), I, in effect, would have been orphaned. So I put myself in the wrong in order to keep and to have love, a fitful, insecure love. I put myself in the wrong in order not to be any more alone than I was. I did not believe them. But I also did not want to believe myself. I longed to believe what they thought was true."

He led me, I really felt him leading me, with his intelligence, his will. I knew positively I was on the right track.

And then it happened.

All this about his wife, Annette—why had he brought it up, lingered over it? I did not believe it was gratuitous. I did not believe it was not meaningful.

But I must be wrong.

I looked at him warily.

"What's wrong?" he asked.

"Nothing. I'm just working something out."

"You're on the right track," he said.

About "Love," the house, that must be what he means, I thought. Not about . . . about . . .

"If your wife weren't going to Vermont the next day, would you consider coming to my party?"

He said carefully, "Probably not. It would be too drastic." What a strange thing to say!

"You mean it's not your practice to mix business and pleasure?"

"Life is full of collisions," he said. An even stranger thing to say!

"My bicycle collided with Edith's up in Nantucket the summer we met. That's *how* we met."

"You see," he said inscrutably.

I felt under great tension. But I was not anxious. I was practically over my anxiety. I did not know what I was suspecting, but I was beginning to be onto something, something I didn't want to know.

"See you next year," he said, making my heart sink. But next year was only two days from then.

"Next year," I said, recovering cheerfully.

I kept an eye on him up to the last moment and then, as I left, closed the door indecisively behind me. What was amiss? What had I left undone, unsaid, unasked? I felt like a diplomat who'd left a dispatch case of highly secret documents behind on a plane, but I felt the way the diplomat felt *before* he'd discovered his loss, before he'd related his sensation of unease to the bag which was not between his body and his crooked arm.

123

I had an agitated, detached three days. I coughed a dry barking cough. I could *not* believe it. Emerson's wife was going up to Vermont for the month of January to work on a project. This fact had a déjà-vu familiarity to it. Nan, whom I did not get to say good-by to, had left for the art colony in Vermont for the month of January to work on her book. Now that she had a contract, she was qualified to attend the colony. "If I want to do it, my husband says I should do it. What's important is what I want to do. He can manage for a month, he says, though I have my serious doubts. Of course, he'll get invitations from our friends and between times scrounge around the kitchen for himself. I won't stay away a day after January thirty-first. I feel guilty enough as it is." That's what she'd told me before that day of my disgraceful misdeed. Attempted misdeed.

I have a built-in familiarity with horror. I live on close terms with it. Therefore I did not trust what I was beginning to suspect. A man who fears burglars every hour doubts himself when he actually hears one entering a second-floor window. I could not believe what I suspected.

That is your problem, I could hear Emerson saying.

There is no escaping him. Dr. Emerson pervades my knowledge of myself—he lives in me. What he had led me to realize about myself I could not escape. My new knowledge was more demanding of my underground self than the police force of the most rigidly totalitarian state. I was my own inquisitor, witness and culprit. But the *j'accuse* I muttered was meant to free me from being a victim of myself.

When I saw him the third day of the new year, he seemed primed for more affable small talk. "I heard from Annette," he said. "She'd just settled into the colony up there, in Vermont. You remember I said she was going to Vermont for the whole month of January?"

I kept my eyes on him. Of course, I had told him about my several terms up there. We colonists referred to our stays as terms, like a stretch of time spent in school or in jail.

I said, "Nan is spending January up there too. Did I happen to mention this to you?" I coughed hard and then got my breath back.

We were playing a lethal hand of poker. His face carefully revealed nothing. "No, you didn't."

"I only knew a few days before seeing you last."

"Did you say good-by to that Nan person?"

"Lately you keep referring to Nan as that Nan person. Why?" I exclaimed as my breathing quickened. I felt disinclined to show him undue respect. I wasn't buying too much from anyone these days. I felt daring, reckless and scared stiff.

"I think," he said, deliberately giving me a literal answer, which I dreaded to hear, "I think it is possibly because I do not believe her name is Nan. Not precisely Nan."

I closed my eyes. I squeezed them tight. I opened them. He was watching me. All my strength left me. After making love a man feels boneless. But I felt weightless, like a kite lolling on its stick feet, waiting for a wind to knock it back or to raise it off the surface of the world. I suppose another way of putting it is I felt faint.

"It can't be!" I whispered. I shut my eyes again. This I really did not want to see.

"You're a grown man, a successful man in your chosen field of work. You must know by now your problem is precisely that believing in yourself feels like taking a risk."

"You know what I'm thinking then?"

"I am not a mind reader," he said at once.

I felt that required a sardonic retort, but I was in no state to make a pertinent one.

"Unfortunately, in this case, I was not a mind reader," he said levelly. "I have never claimed to be one, however."

I started to gag. I stood up, desperate for the bathroom. He pointed to a door behind me, and I ran to it. Inside, I threw up my breakfast and immediately felt much better. I threw up my disbelief. Keeping in a state of disbelief about what I thought of my parents had been a kind of insurance against the knowledge of my own deprivation. But

125

I was a grown man, and I could possess myself only if I believed in myself. Now it was believing in my own perceptions that was giving me the bends.

I sat down in front of him again. "That's why you stopped seeing me so suddenly last summer. God." I had not realized this was true until the moment I voiced it.

"Nan is married to you. What a fool I have been!" I cried. I remembered all I'd told him about my behavior to her, my designs on her, and I curled up inside. I hid my face in my hands.

"There are coincidences in life that are almost too much to accept," he said slowly. "People's lives do collide. Jacqueline Kennedy became a widow because an obscure family failed in their responsibility to a son named Lee. The newspapers are full of the stories of these collisions every day. You could not help it that Annette's office was in your building. I did not know or suspect a thing, with your calling her Nan, and referring to her from the very beginning as a poet and the mother of three. But I, it is I who must and who does assume the full responsibility of having been persuaded to take you back."

I was still in a state of shock. "Who persuaded you?"

"You. You said you were through with her. You said you wanted to finish up your psychotherapy so you would not repeat the same pattern with 'another Nan.' Since you had come far enough along to realize you were acting out some pattern, I took you back. It was my mistake and mine alone. I know perfectly well that acts of will do not change deep compulsions." He struck his forehead.

"You didn't make a mistake. I didn't pursue her, she pursued me," I said to make him feel better. Then I was sorry I said it. She was his wife, and this relationship I had with him was so deeply mixed up nothing I said would ever be right again.

"I wouldn't say she pursued you," he said evenly.

"She called me 'stranger,' indicating she missed me." Something else occurred to me, which I was rather proud of having thought of. I asked, "Did you at any time manipulate me in such a way as to prevent me from . . . from"—this was embarrassing and I saw that

126

our relationship truly had no leg at all to stand on—"succeeding with her?" He could no longer be my doctor, and I could scarcely expect him to consider me a friend. I felt extremely depressed.

"I must remind you I broke off our sessions the morning after I realized who this Nan person was. The day after you told me she was writing a novel, not poetry. Until the week before Christmas and New Year, when you told me, I had no idea you were seeing her again. Today is only January the third."

He had been completely aboveboard. It was I who had tried to be a sneak thief in his bedroom while his flashlight was beamed on me. It was a nightmare of shame and stupidity.

"You played me false!" I cried out, with what I hoped was appropriate anger. I heard my outmoded expression—anger still didn't come too naturally to me.

"I made an error in calculation," he said. "I'm truly sorry. I didn't see it coming. Unforgivable of me! I have spent the last week trying to think how we should proceed now, so that you will not have been set back."

"If you made an error in calculation," I said, "it was not about me. You made one, but it was about Nan. You didn't count on her missing me when I cooled off." I wasn't gallant at all. I was rather perverse, turning my embarrassment against him.

"My wife has demonstrated that she can take care of herself, I'm sure you'll agree."

I still had the lingering suspicion he'd played me false somewhere. Asserting myself, I said so for the second time. "You deceived me!"

He has a certain urbanity. "I could say the same thing to you. Thank heaven, Annette knows what she's doing." He contemplated Nan, who had not strayed, who had been faithful to him. But I could hear her saying to me, "You don't love me at all! I thought you loved me!" I did not remind him of this.

"So Nan Weil is short for Annette Weil," I said.

"Nan Weil," he said musingly. I had never divulged the last name of the married woman I wanted so passionately. "Annette has published poetry under the name of Annette Ungerman, her maiden name. I know she doesn't like the look of that name, its heaviness. I didn't know she'd actually decided to use her mother's name, Weil. By the way, her hair is not auburn. It is gold with copper in it."

"I call it auburn," I said. "But what's wrong with calling herself Annette Emerson?"

"Annette had no adolescence, to simplify a long story. She wants to be someone in herself, to find out who she is. So she is Nan Weil, I see, the novelist. It will look good on her book jacket."

Frankly, I did not feel bad any more. Only a half an hour had passed, but I felt quite settled, not even terribly embarrassed.

He said, "I suggest that we play things by ear for a while. I can't justify it to myself to break off your treatment again so abruptly, yet I should be disbarred from my profession if I continued with you. Think about whether you would like to return to Dr. Ness. I can refer you to someone else, of course. Come in once a week, if you like. While Nan is away, it cannot hurt for us to ease off gradually. But when the first of February comes around, you must have made other plans."

"I would never take up with her again," I declared. "I couldn't now, given how I feel about you."

"Thank you," he said and then shrugged a little deprecatingly. "But a compulsion does not honor promises."

"You are her husband. You could take her away if I started in again."

"Annette is not my property," he said. "Annette is my wife, but she is also a person in her own right. I give her a great deal of privacy, something she'd never had."

"Anyway you can be very sure of her," I reassured him.

"You should know."

We laughed, secure in our knowledge of Nan-Annette, worthy of both of us, and perfect in her disinterested sophistication and wifeliness.

"Annette is also quite a talented writer," her husband said. "I know Nan Weil will produce a first-rate book."

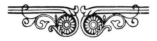

"What do people call you?" I asked him a week later. He didn't understand.

"Do they call you 'Yale'?"

"Can you imagine being called 'Yale' as a child? I'm Herb to everyone," Dr. Yale H. Emerson told me.

That was the last nail I needed in this construction of the truth. Nan had referred to her husband as Herb, no question about it.

"Still working on your problem of belief? Well, let's go into it today."

I was more than eager to. "I can remember someone saying, I think it was one of the housekeepers who came and went in my early years, 'He is only five years old, ma'am.' I remember thinking the housekeeper was referring to me, but I wasn't positive. I do not remember my mother's answer. Once my father lost his temper. It surprised me. I think it shook him too. He swept a whole pile of books onto the floor; a chair fell and one of its legs broke. My mother ran upstairs in this summer house we rented for six or seven years. I cowered in the kitchen looking for the housekeeper, but there was no housekeeper. We hired one only from time to time, depending on my mother's work. I was all alone. My parents were quarreling, but I did not know they were fighting with each other. I thought it must have something to do with me, but what had I done that was wrong? No one told me anything, but it must be my fault.

"The next day I was very tired. My mother told me that if it were not for me, for her little George, they (my parents) would never have any differences in the world. I suspected she was trying to prove to

129

me how much they loved me. But it proved to me they had quarreled because of me, bad me.

"I must have been bad. I must have done something wrong. Tensely, I waited. 'Daddy was wicked to scare you so yesterday,' Mother said. How incredible! I was wrong, but still she loved me. How I loved her in return! When my father came home he apologized to both of us. I was proud and destroyed because he was apologizing to me. Everything was wonderful after that. I was afraid it would end —the peace and the bliss. 'Love heals all,' my mother said, getting ready to go out. She was always going out. My father was rarely home either. I cannot hide from myself any longer that I was a very lonesome kid."

Dr. Emerson said, "Now you are really seeing." He sounded as if he were moved, in a way he'd never let me see before.

I laughed. "I'm a visual artist and I'm just beginning to see. That's a commentary on something or other."

Emerson maintained his attentive silence, and I knew what he was thinking. My life had been devoted to a struggle to see and to make visible. To make visible and, while bringing vision to visibility, to see that its meaning resulted in effect. Effect was all the meaning I ever meant to achieve as an artist. But in my living from day to day, to see would help me to believe. Seeing is believing.

"Words are magical!" I exclaimed. "Words *are* thoughts. Without them you can't think. Words mean so much more than we take them for. In the beginning was the word."

"Your talent has a certain literary aspect to it," he said by rote.

"The more I see what made me, the emotions that made up that little boy which turned into me, the more I believe in me."

"Yes."

"My parents were separated for a year when I was seven or eight. When they got back together (I had been told my mother had to take care of Grandma in Brooklyn), my grandmother moved in with us. She had charge of me, and a new life began."

"You had to learn to see the first seven years clearly."

"You knew all along?"

"There's no magic in any of this," he said modestly. "Have you heard from Annette?"

We looked at each other, each enjoying what the question implied: reality is full of absurdities. He was asking me matter-of-factly if I'd heard from the woman I wanted to seduce, his wife.

"Not even from Nan," I said.

"That's too bad," he said.

"But I didn't expect to hear from her."

Silence.

"Haven't you heard from her?" I asked.

"Of course I've heard from her. She phones. She saves her writing strictly for her novel."

"Isn't everything going well?"

"Being with all those creative people is so stimulating, she's so keyed up, she says, she can hardly get down to work. It's the first time Annette's been in such an atmosphere."

"I remember the first time I was up there. I met Bob Meacham that summer. You know, the fellow who referred me to you in the first place? I was so anxious to be a real live artist, like everyone else, I spent half my time and energy behaving the way real live artists were, I thought, supposed to behave. I had an idea painters were a singular species of individual. I was trying to fulfill an idea that was only in my own head, instead of painting full time. The only thing that makes a painter a painter is painting, rather than doctoring or selling or researching or politicking. Nan will catch on soon."

"I don't think that's her problem," he said. "She's so alive these days, because of the writing, she's too febrile to write."

"Everything is paradoxical. I was so interested in acting out the painter image, I wasn't painting. To me Bob Meacham, who incidentally is up there now, seemed like a businessman that summer. He simply left the breakfast table with a slight chip-on-his-shoulder air and drove to his studio on his motor scooter to get in a day's work. At dinner he seemed liberated and sardonic. Usually a night at the bar in town followed, in the company of a girl or two if he was lucky enough to rustle up two without thick ankles. 'Creative women all have thick ankles,' he used to complain. He's very particular."

"Annette's ankles aren't thick," Dr. Emerson said absent-mindedly.

"They sure aren't."

"But neither is she a foreign princess."

"How did you ever happen to marry a Jewish girl?" I asked him.

"I fell in love."

"But what does 'to fall in love' mean?" I asked him, enjoying my turning the tables on him.

He shrugged, as if to say, This whole situation between Safford and me is out of line, so why act holier than thou at this point? "Falling in love, to me, was finding someone to whom I was physically attracted and who had important qualities I missed in my own background."

"Exoticism? You said Anglo-Saxons are attracted to Mediterranean types because they symbolize the exotic."

"I'm rather conservative in a liberal sort of way," he said. "The qualities Annette has which I wanted to have in my life were warmth, communicativeness, *joie de vivre,* but all combined with a sense of responsibility, a sense of reality. You wouldn't know how responsible she is, how responsible she had to be at too young an age."

"So, as they say, you fell in love."

"And courted her for two years. We went steady for a year before we got married."

"Did you live together?"

"Well," he said, not wanting to be indiscreet. "She doesn't have the mentality of a *jeune fille,* if that's what you mean. I'm sorry to have to put it this way, but Annette probably simply doesn't want you and never will want you."

Now be appropriately angry, I said to myself. But I couldn't be. He was behaving perfectly, as always. He was behaving appropriately with me: man to man, husband to would-be lover.

132

The following week he greeted me with, "I heard from the foreign princess," and waited.

"What's this foreign-princess routine?"

"What does foreign mean to you?"

"Alien, remote, distant, like up in Vermont."

"Good," he said.

"I remember," I said wearily, "I called Nan a foreign princess a long time ago—unattainable, invaluable, above ordinary mortals . . . You seem worried about her."

"I speak to Annette every other evening."

"You could still be worried about her."

"Your mother was always out, you said. Out, far away, unreachable?"

I was still the patient, forking out fifty dollars a session. He was still working on me. It hadn't come to anything else yet. Truthfully, I didn't want him to work on me so conscientiously.

"I am afraid to let go the last metaphor," I said. "In fact, I refuse to."

I had had to take my stand. Taking the stand could also be construed as a new strength. I hoped he'd see it that way.

"Of course," he said.

"You know why I'm afraid," I stated. It was not a question.

"Possibly."

"I cannot bear to live on a single level. My work requires that I continue as I am."

"Your talent may not be vulnerable the way you fear."

"I am so bored with literal reality. I, you, this, that, rent, taxes, birth, death, bills, vacations, success, failure. I have to have this weaving back and forth between the life I lead and the work I create."

"Naturally."

"The life I lead comes to a head, so to speak, in the work I create. The work I create incubates in the life I lead."

"No one questions that."

"I want my intuitions to remain intuitions."

"Why not."

"The metaphors I need can be so easily destroyed simply by stating them too literally."

A silence. "I follow you," he said. "But I do not agree necessarily."

"Because of this Sam Dexter house, I'm going to be written up by Schlossberg, my work treated to depth analysis in *The New Yorker.*"

"Congratulations."

"You know who Schlossberg is?"

"Annette keeps up with him all the time."

"Does Annette know about us?"

"No," her husband said.

A preposterous situation: my asking her husband if the woman I had designs on knew about the confidential relationship we, the two men, had.

"You have never told her? Isn't that strange?"

Dr. Emerson thought for a moment. "It is your analysis. She is an innocent party to it and did not cooperate in"—he put up his hand to prevent my qualifying his statement—"your trying to act out a fantasy. I am not in the habit of mentioning my patients to my wife."

"She never brought me up, that madman downstairs?"

"You were never important to her," he said. But he decided to let me in on something, something I already had inklings of. "She needs to have a sense of being on her own, of being her own person. She left home late, because of the demands of a sick relative. She doesn't want to feel obliged to report to headquarters every little thing that happens. I want her to feel she herself is the only one she is accountable to. To grow, she needs to know I trust her without reservations."

"I still love her, you know," I said.

His face revealed nothing.

"Doesn't it bother you at all?" I asked.

"Her loving you would be another matter," he said.

The next time I saw him was to be the next to the last time. After that I was definitely to have switched to Dr. Ness again. I didn't want Ness, but I'd already established a beginning with him. I simply could not go to a third doctor at this stage of the game.

"I am onto a new idea," I said. "From metaphor I think I'm going on to action."

"You are speaking of your work?"

"Of course."

"You must let me know. You could be speaking of yourself too."

"That's true," I agreed. He definitely understood what was going on in me, on all levels. "See, this Dexter house, as far as I'm concerned, is all done. It's got to be built, assembled, furnished this spring and this summer. But it's done as far as my planning is concerned. I have a new idea, a moving one."

"A touching one?"

"No, something with movement, motion, action in it. Something that you stand on that moves slowly, moves you into a corridor, let's say, of moving pictures flashing by. But because the fleeing scape leaves you, you, the spectator, realize you are traveling a definite road. You are, in relation to the moving away of the other things, sure, taking up a limited space, occupying a definite vantage point."

"Ah," he said.

"Lights flickering, focusing and unfocusing, a chronology of sequence passing under your steady gaze, these and you in it will act together to make a scenic scape."

"Then you need no longer be afraid to let go the last metaphor, since you are now going on to still another," he said pedantically. "It is not the last, after all."

I smiled, sheepish, caught like a boy with syrup on his lips denying he knows where the jam jar is hidden.

"I never feel safe until I'm onto a new idea."

He looked faintly amused, seeming to suggest he'd met my kind before.

"You see what Dexter's 'Love' house is all about? *Was* all about? It was the house of my childhood."

He had actually said that once, hadn't he? Those words exactly. But I had not been ready to put it into these words, to see what these words

135

meant then. To say and to see, to show and to tell, to make the mystery clear. There is nothing invisible. What cannot be made visible does not exist. But the visible remains unseen too often and too long.

"The first five or six years of my life my parents were just settling into their marriage. I had been born within the first year, before my mother was ready to be a mother. She's told me this. She had been an actress, a would-be actress in the big city, as she still calls it, when she met and decided to marry my father. We lived near Poughkeepsie all year, except when my parents took this summer house on the north shore of Long Island, near bay water for me, near a town where there was a summer stock theater for my mother. My father commuted to us weekends only. During the week he kept up his practice at home. When my mother could find a housekeeper in the neighborhood, we had one. I remember a stream of carpetbaggers putting down their giant purses in the kitchen, rummaging in the broom closet for the sacklike smocks they changed into to do the work around the house. My mother was always at rehearsals. She was very beautiful, preparing her hair before leaving and often coming back with makeup still on, theatrical makeup, which she carefully creamed off sitting in front of a makeup table she brought from Poughkeepsie every year. She was really like a princess.

"My father, as I said, was not there during the week. My mother was out rehearsing during the day, while I was taken to the beach or played in the sandbox on the porch. When a play was on, usually Thursday nights through Sunday nights, and occasionally all week long, my mother was away. After supper was the worst time. I would get out of bed, run downstairs and wait by the porch door, in that dim hallway light, until I fell asleep on the floor, until I went out like a light. Loneliness turned me off, made me escape into the nothingness of sleep. To feel nothing, to be nothing was the solution to my longing."

I controlled my tremors as I spoke. My back was tight with tension. Yet in a few minutes a great claw seemed to slip off me, a burden I'd carried for thirty years.

" 'He's only five years old, ma'am,' I remember a woman saying.

"*He* must be me, I thought. I'm the only five-year-old one around here. Everyone else had no personal age and was empowered to lead a life of his own. I was the only one who waited around, never fully satisfied, never believing, even when my mother was home, that her being at home would last. I was afraid to believe and leave myself open to more longing when she left again. Her being there was almost as painful as her absence. It made me just as anxious. She explained to me my father was a busy man. He explained to me my mother was a special, talented person. I understood I was not important, and that they were very good people, full of love and understanding for one another."

"Yes, of course," Dr. Emerson said.

"It is so pat," I protested. "Is it always so pat?"

"Obvious and not obvious. When you created 'The Porch,' could you have told me why?"

"The truth has to come out though, doesn't it, in one form or another?"

"Sometimes it comes out in the manner you mastered. Other times in more destructive form, destructive to the patient or the world. You could have hurt Annette, and yourself indirectly. What precisely were you doing that last time with your Nan?"

It came to me easily. "Acting out my longing and anger against my mother and my father both, but misapplying it. Annette was a foreign princess to me, as my mother was (special and so far away), so I acted for and against a resemblance I assigned her. My father is dead now; it is too late to cope with him, but I must learn to act out my feelings directly with my mother. I am not going to drag any more of her furniture around for her. She can hire someone to do it."

"That's the idea," he said.

"She has us to dinner once a year and I have always brought wine and flowers on this great occasion, buying my way into her life. She's not going to be invited by us until she returns invitations more often."

"You will have to get Edith's cooperation," he said.

I realized what he saw. My change would require adjustments all the way, throughout my life. Edith never even noticed she cooked for my mother several times for each time my mother thought of asking us over. Edith was too selfless—without a strong sense of self. I had not wanted a selfish wife, as I'd told Emerson, so I'd chosen Edith. Everything revealed takes us farther down a road. Every painting painted moves us along to the next painting. Understanding itself creates new problems, but while the problems created by a lack of understanding box one in, my new ones made me feel adventuresome.

"You have been sleeping normally for a month now and eating well," he told me.

"How do you know?"

"You look splendid."

That word made me think of Bob Meacham, my splendid friend, who wanted us to go to Europe with him in March. He was due to leave on the last day of February. We could go now, if it didn't interfere with my Dexter project, for Edith, after all, was no longer pregnant. We would take Amanda with us, of course. If we went, we'd join him March fifteenth and stay a month.

On the first or second day of February I ran into Nan in the delicatessen. She had on a short rose wool dress and knee-high boots. A fox fur hat obscured her auburn hair. I had never seen her look more ravishing—like a Russian princess. I am sorry, but there it was: she did look like a princess and I was not confusing her with my mother any more.

"You're back," I said, settling down at her table. I had to hang up her coat first. Apparently she'd just come in from the outside and not down from her office.

She looked ravishing, but she did not look happy.

"Sit down," she said. I'd already sat myself down.

"Taking a coffee break again?" she asked me. Again? I had not had one today.

"I'm going to have some lunch," I said. It was almost three, and I was famished. Was she distrait or still angry with me about my behavior the last time we'd been together?

"I want to apologize for that . . . that time just before you left," I said.

She did not respond; she looked blank.

I decided to change the subject. "Did everything at the colony go to your liking?" I said awkwardly, placatingly.

"It . . . it . . . wasn't at all what I expected. Actually, it threw me." Unhappiness or displeasure—I could not tell which—colored her tone of voice.

"But you got some work done?"

She was toying with a piece of pie. "I missed having a Jewish pickle now and then," she said with her lips, but her eyes looked past me and the delicatessen. Whatever they saw made them look wounded and receptive to more injury. But the rest of her glowed. The maple wheel chandelier overhead cast a pumpkin-colored light, but the glow Nan wore came from her heart: pearly, dewy, pink and secret. I could barely look at her. I felt I was voyeur to a condition of femaleness, a condition in which struggle and power, in the sense of triumph over a stale self, were locked for an ephemeral moment as in a rose's exaltation before the bloom begins to set and then to fade.

"Which studio did you have?"

"Studio?"

"Which studio did they assign you?" I repeated patiently.

"One right near the main house. I didn't go up with the car. Herb wanted me to take it, but I wanted to be marooned." She laughed unhappily. "I was marooned. I would have been marooned with two cars. The snow in those hills . . ." She shook her head.

"It can be blinding," I said, thinking of the first time I kissed her.

The snow had sealed in that day, bottled it as one's memories are bottled, as perfume is bottled. On wafts of remembered time the sensibilities rove far and deep.

"Blinding!" she exclaimed. "I actually got lost between the main house and Thoreau." Thoreau is the name of a writer's studio on one side of which was a small duck pond. And it is only about a hundred feet from the commons.

She went on. "It's probably better up there in the summer. You can get out more and look around the countryside a bit. And there's less cliquishness if there're more people."

"There're lots more to pick and choose from after the month of May," I said. "Did you get to know Bob Meacham?"

Her lips parted. Her attention swam. I could see her mind was at sea. By will alone, she reined herself in to the present, to me sitting here with her in the half-sour, half-pungent smell of the delicatessen. Sheer concentrating on the literal present must be how spies and double agents maintain their duplicities.

"You know him?"

"I told you about him soon after we met, when, to me, you were still a poet."

"This pie is peculiar," she said, pushing away her plate. "It's stale or something. The food up there wasn't anything to write home about"—she paused over that phrase—"but it is a treat, especially for women, of course, not to have to plan and cook every meal for a change. Of course, the fact of the place itself is a minor miracle. They do so much for you."

"Who else was up there?" I asked to get the lay of the land, so that my speculations might be more accurate.

"Harold Zimmerman, the composer; Natalie Benson, the poet; Amy Jones Tucker, of course; two or three middle-aged painters; and several novelists. Oh, and Steve Hill, who's on the third part of that trilogy of his, and a few other composers whose work I really don't have any idea of."

I ticked them off carefully. Zimmerman is married and unwell.

Everyone knows he's been in a sanatorium recently. Steve Hill is white-haired and a windbag. People avoid him because he's so earnest and so tedious. Amy Jones Tucker always forms a coterie around her of the very young callow artists, whatever their fields, or becomes house mother to the homosexuals. Of the anonymous others, two or three would be dedicated Ping-Pong players after dinner; the others would head for the bar at the 1792 Inn.

"The drinking is heavier in the winter than in the summer," I said.

"Actually, I've got to get back to work," she said, waving to the waitress.

"I'll take care of it."

"Why should you pay for my lunch?" she said. "I'm glad to hear the drinking *is* worse in the winter. There were two who were slightly potted most of the time."

"Does Bob have a beer belly?"

"Bob?"

"Bob Meacham."

She looked up. "I had a tongue sandwich and pie and coffee," she said to the waitress who was adding up her check.

"He's inclined to grossness," I said. I wasn't very nice.

Nan counted out her change carefully and left two dimes and a nickel for the waitress. She put the nickel between the two dimes and tried to even them up in a neat row. She concentrated on making the pattern perfect.

"Between drinking and women," I said, "Bob abuses himself physically. He had this beer belly the last time I saw him. It stuck out to here," and I showed her with my hands. "He's getting to look really middle-aged."

Her eyes, granting me just a brief stare, were hot with a slow burn. "I'll see you," she said, picking up her coat and leaving with great dignity. She seemed to be groping. Yet her groping gave her a dimension, a quality that had not been there before New Year's. She had been a wise child before; now she was a woman with an inkling of how close we walk with chance and accident.

So I was not surprised to find Bob Meacham at home with Edith. I was floored, but I was not surprised.

"Did you get my message?" he asked me at once. He looked fit, I thought, almost without a paunch.

"I regret to say you look splendid," I said, and I noticed Edith was already downing a martini. She never got a head start on me except when Meacham was around.

Edith was putting her hair up these days, paying more attention than usual to herself. I think my new attitudes had an effect on her, unconscious with both of us. Her *sportif* look, when her hair was down and straight, was transformed into a vulnerable hauteur. It was very becoming.

"I called you at the office. You were out to lunch."

"Miss Price flushes messages from you down the john," I told him. "What did you have to say?"

"That I was dropping in tonight, that's all."

"I thought you were going to be in Vermont through February."

"I am, I am. But I had to get away from the white stuff. It gets you down after a while."

"A marooned feeling?"

"The inmates are creepy this time of year. The snow brings out a latent mediocrity. I swear Amy Jones Tucker is going to legally adopt several of the boys. In exchange for mother's cooking, all they have to do is change their names to Tucker, Junior."

"They cook well themselves," Edith said, sticking up for a handy underdog. "They don't need her. She needs them, if you ask me. Her life would be empty except for them. So you needn't be such a bigot, and a dated one too. It would be a pretty dull world if everyone were heterosexual."

"Edith is right," I said. "Who was up there besides the Tuckers?"

142

"The usual assortment of dried nuts and gingery oldsters. Steve Hill is winding up his trilogy and may wear it for a shroud."

"You sound positively dyspeptic today," Edith said.

"No one else was there? No beautiful novelists or poets of the opposite sex?" I asked.

"The winter is no time to go up there," Bob said.

"You're just trying to justify not sticking it out up there and doing your God-intended work, instead of goofing off in New York."

Bob Meacham's eyes are windows to his soul, if by soul we refer to the total experience which is a man. He may be inclined to beefiness, but his eyes are stripped down to listen the way a fisherman fishes. Bob feels, rummaging the world and himself, in order to know what to feel. A poet fishes around and contacts fish called poems. Bob looked at me and came up with information he was not divulging. He knew I was onto something, and I allowed him to know it.

"I'm going back in a day or two," he said.

"Have lunch with me tomorrow," I said.

"At work?" he asked.

"Not here. I work in my place of work."

"You also work here," he argued, suddenly a stickler for facts. "You take part of your rent off here making your scenes."

"Well, how about lunch?"

"I'm having lunch with the Williamses," he said. "I've had this standing invitation with them since Christmas," he lied.

Later that evening in bed Edith and I resolved, after I assured her it would be all right, to go to Europe on March fifteenth and meet Bob in Provence. "I'll get a lot done on 'Love' before we go." Dexter was giving me the help of two carpenters and a mason he retained on his grounds. They could continue without me for a month. "When I get back, I can get right down to the details, which, after all, are what make the house say what it is meant to say.

"I don't want Amanda to be an only child," I added without a break. "Emerson has made me see that." Edith kissed me tenderly.

"We'll work on Junior the moment we get back," she said. "Do you think you'll be through with all that analysis soon?"

"I've got the structure of the problem figured out. I possibly still need to do a little housekeeping," I said, thinking, I still can't get away from the "house," it seems. Housekeeping of different varieties comes up every day and must be attended to.

"I knew you'd resolve your problem just the way you have," Edith said, giving me quite a start. "Why are you so surprised? I'm not dumb."

"I know you're not dumb. But what do you mean, resolve—"

"This new thing you're working on is a fascinating new direction. You're too close to see it. But I'm not too close."

In my workroom at home I'd begun to work on steel sheets. My motion idea I was going to work on at the office. It required a lot of space, and I was moving Party Packages to a warehouse I'd found in the Nineties between First and York. It looked as if from now on I'd work on my steel sheets at home and on the motion-screen object on Fifty-fourth Street.

I was leaving metaphors not only for movement, as I'd told Emerson, but also for self-images. I got the idea while shaving one morning. Every time we see ourselves in a mirror we see a portrait of ourselves framed by the medicine cabinet.

So far I've only done an image of my face. I've pasted a painted paper collage of half my face on the right side of an oval sheet of steel. When I present myself to the sheet, the blank half is filled with my reflection. Which, I ask, is more real, my reflected half or my painted self? Which is art?

Am I a kind of surrealist with my waking dreams? Do I understand that word correctly? As I've said before, I've never been able to decide for sure if reality seemed too real to me or not real enough. But I think I do know that the making of art seems very real at the time it is going on. Its unquestionable reality is a boon, a gift, an insurance policy against the ambiguities of guilts and acts, the fables of personal history. The moment a work is accomplished and becomes a part of reality, it surrenders me to doubt again. This is why I must keep producing.

I started to cough when I suspected that Emerson was Nan's husband. Horror clouded my breathing. I was mirrored in reality, caught in the act in a reflection. Plate glass reveals streetlights marching up Third Avenue, but the same glass also imposes lamplight, in which one leans against a cushion, onto the image of the city lights outside. I saw through myself with Dr. Emerson. And by some sleight of hand realized I was real.

I had had no place in my parents' lives, contrary to what they maintained. I buried my anger and blinded myself to their shams, but I vowed to show them I counted. I could have avenged myself by becoming a successful anything, a scientist, a tycoon, a politician. But I showed them by making something to be seen, to be looked at, to be displayed before their eyes. I became an artist.

I believe in my autonomous self more now than ever before. It is a precious condition to be in, to own—beyond any other worldly value. To thy self be true. The self that shadowed Nan and picked through her garbage was true to that ancient self, compelled by its need to any end, even destruction through self-immolation. But to my new self I am now true. I see that, and I am happy.

Life unreels like fiction. I waited for a month for Bob Meacham to tell me why he drove down to New York four times, making the trip during the week only, hanging around the apartment, not my office, making even Edith, who knew nothing at all, say, "You've got spring fever and I'm still wearing my fur coat. If you aren't getting any work done up there, why don't you decide to stay with us until you leave for France?"

"I've got to get the book done. They're waiting for it."

She didn't say, You can't get it done barging in on us at all hours. I don't think she noticed that Bob didn't hang around during the day. Edith said he was always at the door around five, however, his arms full of wine or rich desserts or flowers. He felt guilty about something and tried so hard not to impose on us. He paid his way with gifts and conversation, and slept on a cot in my workroom. Edith absolutely forbade him to bring us anything more.

He never breathed a word to us about why he was in New York so often. He too is a discreet man. Frankly, I must say it surprised me how honorable he is. It made me think I should revise my idea of his Lothario reputation. Either he was amorous and straitlaced, or he was less amorous than I hoped. Don't we all need a friend who vicariously acts out fantasies we are too timid to pursue?

I waited all month, but Bob told me nothing I didn't already know. Nan was not working. Whenever he was in town, she arrived at the office early and left at eleven. At four she returned and left for home half an hour later. I wondered why she came in at all. I wondered if they met at the public library to hold hands or were at the Williamses', both of whom went out to work all day.

Nan had a wild look. She was not enjoying herself, whatever she was engaged in. She was going through some necessary suffering. She seemed angry with herself and still, oh still, in full bloom like a rose on its day of perfection.

I have a certain nasty streak. She liked Bob better than me, and I am only human after all. I had referred to Bob's beer belly; I made the remark that drink and women were ruining him physically. Un-called-for remarks. Unkind comments. I made another one when I passed her on the landing one day.

"I understand time is of the essence." That's all I said.

She stopped. As if I'd put my finger on a painful bruise, her eyes welled with tears. Her mouth was tightly closed.

"I didn't mean anything by it," I said. "Truly." I was really sorry.

"You don't know what you're talking about," she said.

"Your book. Your novel is about time. And you are making up for lost time getting it written after all those years when you had to moonlight at dull jobs."

She looked at me bitterly.

"Don't talk about things you know nothing about," she said and continued down the stairs, to meet him (?), to make love with him (?), to live all she could before March first when he left? No one said he had to leave. Yet he'd declared rather vehemently he was leaving as planned, as if he were being forced to, whether his book was finished or not.

"I can always finish it long distance. Publishers don't like it, but it can be done," he stated.

"You can always come back," I said.

"Coming back to it," he said, his eyes rummaging through mine to see what I'd meant, "may help. I mean, leaving it for a while may give everyone a new perspective on it."

"The publisher too?" I asked innocently.

Suddenly I wondered if she'd told him about me, about my behavior. But I didn't think so. She was a married woman, and one so torn, so unhappy with her need for him, he was honoring only her plight by his discretion. March arrived and Bob left New York as scheduled.

The breaking up of winter leaves the atmosphere chaotic and gusty. In August riots and wars break out, but in March the spirit is simply disorderly. Nan walked up and down the stairs and drank her coffee in the delicatessen, quietly, demurely deranged. She was not present. She was living beside herself, her life somehow continuing in her stead.

Emerson telephoned me one day the second week of March. He first asked, "How are things going?"

"Very well. And with you?"

"You haven't taken up with Dr. Ness yet?" he asked, knowing full well I hadn't.

"When I get back from Europe April fifteenth, I'll get in touch with him. It seemed pointless to start in and leave after a session or two."

"Would you join me for lunch tomorrow?" he asked me.

"Why yes," I said, surprised. "Of course."

"At the Museum of Modern Art? In the members' dining room."

"Fine."

"One o'clock tomorrow," and he hung up.

The shoe, I thought, is on the other foot, is it not? It was entirely immature of me to be so utterly incredulous. Incredulous equally that he had called me at all and that he was a member of the museum. Yale Herbert Emerson is a human being, I reminded myself. He's a human, human being, who owns two paintings which I've seen. Why shouldn't he be a member of the museum?

I arrived first and took a corner table by the deck outside. I saw him coming, and he seemed shorter in this setting. No shorter than I, but no taller. In his office he was beyond considerations of size.

He sat down and put his napkin on his lap. He seemed quite puritanical, something I'd never noticed before. Quite square, in this setting. Not so human as fallible. Not so fallible as susceptible— susceptible to germs, fluctuations of the stock market, the pain of love, the fear of dying. Just like any other person I might be having lunch with.

We made small talk, in the manner to which we had become accustomed, only we made small talk about how I felt, how my new work was going, how the "house" was progressing.

"I'm going to get involved with another house," I said.

"You aren't going on to motion?"

"Motion and images, both. What I mean is Edith and I have decided to build a summer home on the Island. I'm actually looking forward to it, and you know I'd originally wanted to get involved only for Amanda's sake. Children need the country. But I don't think I'm an exclusively urban person any more, thanks to you. We've already been out looking for property. We're leaving for France next Tuesday."

The small talk ended. I let the silence accumulate. *I* was not the one to bring up Bob Meacham. Nan would certainly not have told him. I didn't think it had come to that, or she would not be suffering so.

"Has Edith quite recovered from her miscarriage?" he asked.

"Yes, but she needs this vacation probably more than I do. We're going to try again soon. We don't want Amanda to be an only child." Then I saw an opening. "Do you have children?"

"No."

I waited.

"We are in the works to adopt," he said. "The agencies scrutinize prospective parents very carefully, but we've been given the hope that within the year they may have a baby for us. Annette wants to have finished her novel before the infant arrives, which, once they've cleared us, can be at any time. We are already considered old prospects by the agency. They naturally prefer younger parents. She is under great pressure over this time element."

"That accounts for a lot, doesn't it?"

"Time preys on her. Too many years of her life were literally consumed by her family." But he seemed to be avoiding, putting off really saying what he wanted to say. Why had he wanted to have lunch with me? But though he knew me as no one else in this world did, that tied me to him, that did not tie him to me, I reminded myself.

"I shouldn't ask," he then said, bracing himself, "but is Annette getting any work done these days?"

I did not look him in the eyes. I wanted to help him preserve his dignity.

"How would I know? Why don't you ask her?"

He thought for a moment. "She's been strange. I *have* asked her how the book is coming. Once right after she got back from Vermont. The second time, the night before last. She burst into tears and I found her in the bathroom crying her heart out."

"Writers have blocks," I said easily. "I understand they can get very desperate over them."

"Yes, of course," he said, grateful. Now who was glad to take a crumb of comfort? "That must be it."

"There was a writer up at the colony one year who discovered he couldn't work in the country. He came all the way from San Francisco to discover he couldn't work in the woods. He tried to set fire to his studio bed. How's that for despair?"

"That extreme!" he said, thinking about something else.

"Painters have packed up and left because the color of the trees cast a sickly tinge on their palettes. Composers have been driven mad because of the chirping birds."

He sighed. "Sometimes I wish she'd never gone up there."

"It will pass," I said.

His eyes caught mine, but I was the first to look away.

"How do *you* feel about her now?" The emphasis on the *you* made my eyes flicker. Then he'd guessed there was someone else. Or was I imagining this? I also suspected he had an ax to grind. Or am I crazy, I thought. Perhaps he wanted me to distract her from more dangerous people. After all, I was married and not free. Others might be single and more importunate. After all, I also understood my own motivations, and so my drives were qualified.

"Your wife is a beautiful girl emerging into a beautiful woman, but I have no designs on her any more. I'm sorry. You see, you were entirely right in your diagnosis. My passion and my desperate need of her have gone up in smoke."

"But it will not pass unless she goes through it," he said. There was no question that he understood what was happening with Annette.

"I'm sorry I can be of no use," I said.

He closed his eyes briefly, thinking something through.

"If there is anything I can do in any other way . . ." I said.

"I believe," he said, "the block, this block of hers, will pass. And she'll be writing soon again."

I was coughing quite a lot through my dessert and coffee. I felt there was something satanic in the way life read, like a bad story you could not rewrite, unfolding. The sick and the well must take life as

150

it comes. Life itself has a sick, a sickening, quality.

There was a moistness in his eyes due, I'm sure, to his contact lenses.

"I wish she did not feel so guilty about it," he said unexpectedly.

I did not want him to think I knew. I did not want to see through any more plate glass windows supplied by him. I said, "She was only away a month, certainly she shouldn't feel guilty about it. She might have stayed away another month. If it's as important to her to get this novel done as it seems to be, what's an extra month? But she stayed away only one month."

He seemed more cheerful then. And I was cheered for him. It was true. Nan could have extended her stay. But she had chosen not to. She had not wanted to stay away from him two months. She was free but responsible, conscientious though awakened.

"Sometimes I think she's perfect," he said.

"Both of you are," I said impulsively, foolishly. But why not say it? I felt like saying it. "Writers' blocks leave as mysteriously as they come."

"She must go through it, you are right."

He had said that, not I. "But you knew that all along."

"Still," he said, "it helps to talk to someone about it."

"She will come through fine," I said. "She is a true and honest writer." Bob Meacham would be in Europe for the rest of his sabbatical. Edith and Amanda and I would be with him for a while. I too believed it would pass.

"Let's look at some of the photographs downstairs," he said. "I'm in the mood for the glimpses of life that photographers see so clearly."

"The visible," I said.

"Even the visible has to be made accessible," he said as we went down in the elevator to the photographic exhibit.

But some things are survived better when they are left unseen, I thought. I mean only that discretion has its social uses.

I may have misread it all. Nan had said nothing to me. Bob had been tight-lipped. What had Emerson talked about anyway? Most of that palaver about writers' blocks I'd supplied. I could be all wrong. That's reality. Not everything is down in writing. But I believe I'm right.

Given that my mad passion has disappeared, after our vacation I may go back to Emerson. There is nothing now to prevent it. I see, I see, but I still have things to discuss. Aspects of aspects, infinite in a world without end.

"I believe it will pass," he said. My heart goes out to him.

Belief is creative. To believe that his wife will end her affair is his act of love. His life is based on that faith. To believe is an act, as a blindfolded man about to grasp a trapeze swung at him a hundred feet above the ground acts and is part of an act at a circus. Decisions taken create our lives. Emerson is allowing his wife to find out something about herself, to act out an experience she may never have had and did not know she missed until she met Bob Meacham. He is writing his own life, by deciding to wait out her crisis, as much as she is writing a novel.

To believe is to realize. To make real.

My real head reels. I am not a writer, but in writing this down, in getting this off my chest, I have become a writer. I have novelized my life, and a transitory aspect of theirs—Nan's, Bob's, my wife's and my doctor's.

We are still writing out our lives. I had to have in writing the story of my analysis and the bizarre triangle in it to dispel its absurdity. My cough, by the way, occurs only occasionally now. I have projected myself both to Emerson in his office and onto these pages. I have, in a sense, invented me. The "I" that life invented thirty-seven years ago creates its own protagonist—relaxed now—living his own life story, as I, George P. Safford, keep on coughing and breathing, wonderingly.

I wonder: Will Bob still be in Provence when we arrive there next week? Or will his third book of poems sooner or later need working on here, after all? In April, May or perhaps in June—before Annette will have really returned home to Herb Emerson?

All anyone can do is wait and see.

74 75 76 77 10 9 8 7 6 5 4 3 2 1